LANCOTHY

LANCOTHY

SOUL STONE MAGE BOOK SIX

SARAH NOFFKE   MARTHA CARR   MICHAEL ANDERLE

DISRUPTIVE IMAGINATION®

Lancothy Team
JIT Beta Readers

Micky Cocker
Kelly O'Donnell
Larry Omans
Paul Westman
Edward Rosenfeld
James Caplan
Thomas Ogden
Alex Wilson
John Ashmore
Timothy Bischoff
Alex Wilson

If we missed anyone, please let us know!

Editor
Jen McDonnell

L oud ticking echoed through the rustic foyer of the abandoned boarding school. At one time the building had been full of laughter and the bustling feet of precocious pupils. Still, even with the fine layer of dust covering the stone banister and tile floor, its original charm seeped through.

"The realtor who showed it to me said the building is haunted." Cordelia said, turning to face Hamilton. He didn't look impressed as he ran his finger over a large vase sitting on the floor by the entry way. Hamilton was wearing his usual suit and the scowl made him look quite cute, but that was only because Cordelia found the more hostile emotions attractive. A smile made his green eyes light up, but a grimace made his power flow from his gaze.

"Haunted, huh?" Hamilton asked. "We're vampires...the thing of nightmares. Aren't *we* the ones who haunt?"

"We both know ghosts aren't real," Cordelia said, looking at the large grandfather clock against the wall that was responsible for the loud ticking sound. It was nearly morning. They'd have to take refuge in the basement, since proper curtains hadn't yet been installed over the floor-to-ceiling windows. The center atrium was also a gigantic problem with its huge skylight. Humans loved their sun, Cordelia thought with major irritation.

"Are any of the old students of this boarding school still roaming the grounds?" Hamilton asked, not looking amused. "I'm hungry."

"We'll feed in a bit," Cordelia said, striding over to Hamilton. Today she wore one of her favorite red dresses. All her dresses were red. Why would she wear anything but? This one had a heart-shaped neckline, and ruffles that spilled all the way to the floor. It was heavy, but that wasn't a problem for Cordelia with her incredible strength. She ran her fingernail down Hamilton's lapel. "Do you like the house?"

Hamilton eyed the dusty foyer, disgust making his lip curl. His gaze softened when it landed on Cordelia. "No, not really. But I like you, and you picked it."

"It's not our forever home," Cordelia explained. "It's just a base of operations for the brood until we find something better."

Hamilton sniffed. The air in the old boarding school was stale, and laced with what Cordelia had hidden in the closet—a sort of housewarming present for her love. "You know I don't mean any offense to your efforts. I'm just picky."

Cordelia leaned into Hamilton and her lips grazed the side of his neck. Her fangs instinctively emerged, her desire for blood linked to her lust for the man before her. "I enjoy that you're selective. You picked me, didn't you?"

Hamilton's hands gripped Cordelia's hips, and he pulled her in close. "I would have no other."

A cough sliced the air, interrupting the couple, and Cordelia pulled back but didn't turn away. "Yes, Ata?" she asked, her tone impatient.

"Using the tracking spell, I think I've located a page from the *Book of Dead*," Ata said.

This stole Cordelia's attention. She turned to look up at the wizard, who stood at the halfway point on the long staircase. He was dressed in the traditional robes of the New Egypt coven, and held his crook lightly in his fingers. Since the disturbance with the queen of Virgo, Azure, he'd been a bit more difficult to control. A wizard, even one as powerful as he, couldn't resist the vampires' mind control entirely, but he could fight it. Cordelia worried that he'd find a way of breaking it.

More importantly, she worried that the pages of the *Book of the Dead* would surface. Centuries ago the earliest founder vampires had stolen the pages that detailed how to eradicate vampires or cure vampirism. They couldn't be destroyed, but they could be lost—and they had been for a long time. With vampirism now spreading in the homeland of New Egypt, it was crucial that the pages be found and kept away from Chibale and his coven.

"Do tell," Cordelia said, her eyebrow arched in curiosity.

"The queen of Virgo has it," Ata stated, his voice neutral. He appeared almost like a statue with his black hair pulled back in a ponytail and his jaw firm. The swirling tattoos that covered his legs, arms, and face were less visible in the darkened house.

"What? When did she get it?" Hamilton asked, stepping forward.

"My spell doesn't tell me when, only that she's in possession of one of the pages," Ata said.

Cordelia gritted her teeth and stomped her black heel on the stone floor. "Damn that witch. She escaped from us, and now has a page that could spell our demise."

"I knew she was going to be trouble," Hamilton said, his eyes steaming with fury.

"She won't be a problem when we turn everyone in her kingdom into vampires," Cordelia said. "She'll be begging us to turn her then."

"And we won't," Hamilton said. "That will be her punishment."

"You're so cruel, my love." A wicked smile sprang to Cordelia's face. "I happen to think that she'd make a fine founder, and I could use a formidable female companion."

Hamilton gawked at Cordelia, his eyebrows knitted together. "You have me. Why do you need another companion?"

Cordelia brushed a hand over Hamilton's firm jaw. "You're wonderful, but every woman needs another female who can relate to her. I've yet to find one intriguing enough to turn into a founder."

"Yes, and soon we will have a population of bats. We need to decide how to use them," Hamilton stated. Lux and Devo had already set out for Lancothy to retrieve as many bats as they could so that the mission to create founder vampires could be completed successfully. Hamilton and

Cordelia had only created a handful of follower vampires to date, and they'd need to expand their efforts to ensure their brood thrived. Vampires were truly powerful in numbers, and taking over New Egypt was their ultimate goal.

"I guess," Hamilton said, a look of disapproval on his face.

Cordelia's heart was lightened by Hamilton's jealousy. Proudly she turned back to Ata. "I want you to try another tracking spell. We *must* find those other pages. How many are there?"

"I'm not certain…maybe three or four?" Ata said.

"We need all of them. But *we* can't touch the queen, so instead I want you to create something that can go after her," Cordelia ordered.

"Yes," Ata said with a bit of hesitation in his eyes.

"Yes, what?" Cordelia asked.

"Yes, Master," he said, his voice sounding dead.

"That's better. Off you go." Cordelia returned her attention to Hamilton. "Now, I say that we christen this house the right way."

A heated look crossed Hamilton's face. "What do you have in mind?"

Cordelia peeled away from her lover and crossed the foyer to the closet door. The handle was rusted, but could still be turned with a bit of effort. When she pulled back the door, there was a man standing in the empty space. His gaze was dull, and his mouth hung open like he was in a trance.

"The realtor didn't just help us find this location, but is also going to be our first meal in the place," Cordelia told Hamilton. "Come forward," she commanded the man.

Moving like a robot, the man marched out of the closet where she'd made him stay, using the slightest bit of effort with her mind control.

"Halt," she said when he stood between Hamilton and her. Cordelia brushed the side of the man's neck and a moment later found that Hamilton had joined her on the other side, using his super-speed.

"What a great idea you had. I always enjoy feeding with you, my love," Hamilton said.

"Yes, I know." Cordelia reared her head back and her fangs slid into place, then she sank them into the realtor's neck. Hamilton did the same on his side, and the two drank until they were full and the man was dead.

1

"Would you like a date?" Ever asked. He was sitting on the long sofa next to Azure.

She looked up, distracted. In his fingers, Ever was holding a shriveled date he'd picked up from the bowl on the side table, and Azure grimaced with disgust at the fruit. "Hell, no. Those things are disgusting. They should be outlawed."

Ever smiled and popped it into his mouth, chewing. "They're definitely not chocolate cake, but they suffice when hunger strikes."

"When are we going to dinner?" Monet asked. He was lying on the couch opposite them and tossing a red foam ball into the air.

"Soon," Azure said, stirring the contents of the scrying bowl. "We need to get back before it's dark."

"So the evil bloodthirsty zombies plaguing the streets of New Egypt don't eat us," Monet added.

"They aren't zombies, they are vampires," Azure said. "And it's so they don't bite one of you. *I'll* be fine."

Monet caught the ball just before it careened into his face. He paused for a moment to eye the ruby she now wore to protect her from vampires before he threw it into the air again. "Yeah, I'm glad soul stones aren't red. It would totally clash with my hair."

"You'd look very Christmas-y," Ever said, pointing to the lavender amethyst Monet wore on a leather band around his wrist.

Monet's face scrunched in curiosity. "What's 'Christmas?'"

Ever laughed. "It's a thing on Earth—a celebration where you exchange presents. I'll take you sometime. You'll like eggnog.

"Presents!" Monet exclaimed. "I'm game. Let's bring this holiday over to Oriceran. What's it all about?"

"There was this man named Jesus—"

Azure waved Ever off. "Earth lessons later. I've finally gotten the bowl to work, so Gran should be coming through soon."

Everyone inside the large carriage fell silent except Laurel, who was cuddled into a ball in a neighboring armchair. She hadn't been sleeping well, so she had been taking catnaps lately. The werecat hadn't appreciated the expression, but had merely frowned when it was mentioned.

Monet picked up his wand from the side of the couch and pointed it at the werecat, who was snoring and purring slightly. When a brief gust of wind hit Laurel she awakened with a start and looked around in confusion, wondering what had woken her. Monet resumed throwing the ball and tried to look innocent.

"Gran, are you there?" Azure asked.

Gran's wrinkled face swam into view on the surface of the scrying liquid. "Child, excuse my French, but what in Merlin's beard are you thinking? For the love of shriveled pig's liver, get the troll's head out of New Egypt."

"What's 'French?'" Monet asked, holding the red ball just above his head. "And Sari, that's what you're calling cursing these days?"

"Shut the hell up, Monet," Gran fired back.

Azure smiled, nostalgia blossoming in her chest for Virgo and her family. "I miss you too, Gran."

The old woman shook her head of lavender hair and her scowl deepened. "This is not about missing you. Gillian tells me there are vampires in New Egypt. You're not safe!"

"Did Gillian also tell you that Mage Lenore gave me a necklace that protects me from vampires?" Azure asked.

Gran narrowed her eyes, focusing on the ruby hanging around Azure's neck. "Yes, and that's very curious. That old bat is sneaky as hell. Do you know if it really works?"

Monet laughed. "Sari, you calling anyone 'old and sneaky' is ironic."

Ever nodded. "She's right, though."

"Yeah, those two women are made from the same yarn," Monet said, continuing to toss the red ball up. Laurel was instantly entranced, watching the ball fly up and then drop.

Azure shook her head, trying to focus despite the many distractions. "The necklace does work. These founder vampires tried to turn me, but couldn't because of the protection. And they couldn't get it off me, either."

"Muddy frog's feet!" Gran screamed. "Child, I can't believe you've been playing with vampires. Do you have no sense at all?"

"I wasn't playing with them," Azure explained. "They abducted me."

Gran threw both her hands to her cheeks and took in a few ragged breaths. "Are you trying to kill an old witch?"

"No, not at all, Gran," Azure said, suddenly feeling guilty for causing her grandmother any distress. It was rare for the old witch to show concern like this, which just proved how dangerous the vampire epidemic was. "You don't have to worry. I'm safe."

"What about Monet and Ever?" she asked.

"Thanks for the concern," Finswick said, hopping onto the table and peering into the scrying bowl. His white-tipped black tail jerked violently.

Her expression softened at the sight of the cat. "Oh, I bet you're loving this, Fin. Vampires on your first big adventure. Good for you." Her gaze returned to Azure. "But seriously, what about those other guys?"

Laurel tore her gaze from the ball and looked down at Manx, who was chewing happily on a bone in his black dog form. "Are you getting tired of being dismissed?"

The dog looked up and blinked his bright eyes. "Not really. We're not in any danger. I mean the vampires could bite us and kill us, but we're not going to turn into the beasts."

"Mmm," Laurel mused, returning her attention to the ball Monet was tossing. Manx was also distracted by the movement now that he'd noticed it.

"Gran cares about me," Monet sang.

"I do not," Gran spat, "but I promised your mother on her deathbed that I'd look after you. I know how spiteful that evil witch was, and she'd probably haunt me if I didn't deliver on my promise."

Monet had become an orphan at a young age when his mother died from a breast enhancement charm that went wrong. She'd fallen sick immediately afterwards and called the queen mother to her deathbed. Nothing could have been done for the witch, although since then Monet had created a potion that would have saved his mother. It was a sad irony. Since his father had also disappeared long ago, Gran had also been his pseudo-grandmother, pretending she didn't care for Monet but in reality harboring a deep affection for him.

"Gran, we're safe in the carriage," said Azure, gesturing to the large vehicle which had been serving as their residence since the hotel room was destroyed. Oak had even enlarged the inside of the carriage to include a private bedroom for Azure and Laurel, saying that females needed space away from boys. He apparently didn't like the idea of the girls sleeping in the same room with Monet and Ever.

"The carriage is badass, by the way," Monet said.

"I know that," Gran spat. "You all would have figured that out earlier if you had taken the carriage instead of those flea-ridden horses."

"Well, you're always right. We should have listened to you, old woman," Monet said, tossing the ball down the long stretch between the sitting area and the door. Manx sprinted after it.

Gran craned her neck as if trying to see someone. "Where is Ever? Is he there with you?"

"I'm here," Ever said, moving closer to Azure and staring down into the bowl. "How are you, Sari?"

She smiled, her eyes lighting up. "Can you convince my-granddaughter-the-queen to return to Virgo so you don't lose your magic and become a vampire? You'd be useless to me then."

Ever blinked with surprise, looking speechless.

"Now you know that Sari's love is conditional," Monet said. Manx had returned with the slobbery ball and now rested his head on the sofa next to Monet, begging him to toss it again.

"I don't think I can *make* Azure do anything, and you know that," Ever said, looking down into the bowl.

"Gran, I have a page from the *Book of the Dead*." Azure shooed Finswick off the ancient piece of paper that was covered with hieroglyphs. She held it up, careful to keep it away from the scrying liquid.

"Sizzling goats' brains! You're not serious?" Gran exclaimed.

Monet giggled. "You watch your mouth, Gran."

"Where did you get that?" she asked, her lavender eyes wide with shock.

"I found it on Earth in the Sphinx," Azure said in a bored voice, as if this weren't at all bizarre.

"When we spoke with Gillian," Ever chimed in, "he said he might be able to decipher it. Can we send it to you via Manx?"

"You might be nice to look at, but you're an idiot, Ever," Gran said.

"Thank you...I think," Ever replied, his tone light.

Azure looked at Ever. With his jet-black hair, blue eyes,

and pointy ears, he was quite a sight to look at. Too often she'd watched women gawk at the Light Elf when they were in public. However, lately it was Ever who couldn't seem to take his eyes off Azure. Ever since she'd returned from being abducted, covered in blood, he'd been more concerned for her, even though she had the protective amulet.

"That page from the *Book of the Dead* might include a way to end vampirism," Gran said. "That's the reason the original founders stole the pages in the first place. We can't entrust it to a pooka to deliver."

Manx dropped the ball from his mouth and morphed into a black goat. "*Maw*! I take offense to that."

"What are you going to do, eat my shoes? Oh, wait… you already did that," Gran said, looking off to the side as if she could see Manx, then she returned her gaze to Azure. "It appears you're going to have to come back to Virgo. We need to decipher that page. This might be the key, although I know there's more than one page."

Azure shook her head. "I can't, Gran. I promised the coven here that I would help. And more importantly, there's a witch who has been turned and a wizard who is under the control of the vampires. I'm going to help them."

"Sari, do you think Gillian could decipher the page through the scrying bowl?" Ever asked.

Sari looked at something to the side and muttering filled the air. "He said no."

"He's there?" Azure asked.

"I'm here," Gillian called. "I'm not certain I can decipher the page at all. Someone in the Light Elf Library might be able to, but if they find out we have it they'll confiscate the page."

"That's rude," Laurel said. "They don't own it."

"But they own the book," Gillian said. "I really need to study the page in person."

"I'm not sure how to get it to you," Azure said. "We're setting off for Lancothy almost immediately. The vampires are hunting for bats, and we need to cut them off."

"You're *what*?" Gran asked, her face flushing red. "Send Monet and Ever back with the page. We can't risk those two getting turned."

"I'm not leaving Azure," Monet said, sitting up and peering out the carriage window, which ran from the floor to the ceiling.

"Me either," Ever said, shaking his head.

"Azure, you have some loyal mutts," Gran said, and looked to the side again, probably at Gillian. "That's a fine idea. That's what I like about you, Gillian…you actually think."

"What did he say?" Azure asked.

"He proposes that we meet you on the Mountain of Truth, which is on your way to Lancothy," Gran said. "Mage Lenore might be able to offer some help on this debacle."

"Do you think she can decipher the page, or might have answers about how to cure vampirism?" Azure asked.

"Dear Azure," Gran began, "I'm fairly certain that Mage Lenore has the answer to almost everything, but she always wants us to figure it out on our own. That ornery witch won't give us a shortcut to save her damn life."

"Okay, then we'll meet you on the Mountain of Truth,"

Azure said. It would be good to find out why Mage Lenore had given her the protective ruby. Well, her cousin, a batty old witch, had been the one to give it to Azure, but it had come from Mage Lenore.

"How are you going to find your way up the Mountain of Truth?" Ever asked.

Sari looked in Gillian's direction once more. "Yes, I know they're silly children who have no clue." She looked back at Ever. "Don't you worry, young 'un. We will be there."

Azure glanced sideways at Ever. "You *are* a young 'un, aren't you? Monet and I have like seventy-five years on you."

"Fifty," Ever corrected.

"Which, for magical beings, pretty much makes you two the same age," Gran said. "You were born in the same century, which is all that matters."

"Matters for what?" Azure asked.

"Never mind that for now, child," Gran said.

"The sun is setting. Unless we're ordering pizza then we'd better get to dinner," Monet said.

"All you think about is your stomach," Gran snapped, pursing her lips in disapproval.

"I actually care about not getting bitten, since the bloody beasts prowl at night," Monet retorted.

"Oh, well, that's a valid point," Gran replied. "Don't get yourself turned, Monet Torrance, or I'll have your head."

"Yes, ma'am." Monet winked at Azure and then whispered, "She loves me."

"I do not," Gran retorted in a sing-songy voice, then swiped her wand over the scrying bowl and disappeared.

2

Sari drew in a breath as she stepped away from her scrying bowl, which stood on a pedestal in her study. She turned to find Reynolds standing behind her and wearing a ridiculous look of disapproval. The wizard still had a full head of red hair although he was a little older than her. The red goatee clashed horribly with his purple soul stone, that he wore in a ring on his middle finger.

"Did I hear that correctly? You're going to the Mountain of Truth when there's been an outbreak of vampirism?" Reynolds asked.

Sari's gaze fell on the gnome, who was hunched oddly over a book that was larger than him. He was studying up on Egyptian hieroglyphs. Ignoring Reynolds' question, she said to Gillian, "Are you all right with leaving the Potions Shop for this?"

Gillian pulled off his brown bowler hat and scratched his head, which only had a small patch of orange hair on it. He had more hair growing out of his ears than he did on his head, but didn't like to be reminded of it. "It should be fine. Since Monet left I don't get much business. I just need to have Finnegan restock for me, and we'll go on the honesty policy for customers."

"Sari, are you going to answer my question?" Reynolds demanded.

Sari turned to Reynolds slowly, her face pinched with irritation. "I was under the impression that you were here to borrow a book. Why then does it appear that you're spying on me and butting into my affairs?"

"Pardon me for being concerned for your wellbeing," Reynolds snapped, turning his attention back to the shelves of books. The Light Elf Library was impressive in its sheer number of volumes, but Sari had numerous rare books in this oversized study—ones that weren't just *about* magic, but *were* magical.

Reynolds muttered under his breath as he ran his fingers over the spines of some books in front of him.

"What was that, Reynolds?" Sari asked, biting off each word.

He turned, looking surprised. "What? Oh, nothing. I was just remarking about how irresponsible it is to trample off to the Mountain of Truth on your own when there are vampires on the loose."

"Irresponsible?" Sari yelled, her face flushing hot. "I wasn't the one who got himself turned into a statue for Merlin-knows-what."

"It was a misunderstanding." Reynolds waved her off.

Gillian swiveled his attention back to Sari, still waiting for her response.

"A misunderstanding that left you a statue? You'd still be like that if it weren't for the queen," Sari scolded.

Reynolds hung his head in shame. "I'm well aware of that, but just because I made a mistake doesn't mean that you should as well."

Sari gaped in fury. "*Mistake*? Assisting the queen isn't a *mistake*. It is my duty as the queen mother and her grandmother."

Gillian turned his attention to Reynolds, shamelessly eavesdropping. A worm slipped from the page of the giant book and reached for Gillian's face.

"Well, if you insist on going then I'm accompanying you," Reynold said.

Sari balled up her fists and was about to stomp her feet, but paused and turned her attention fully to Gillian. "You might want to turn the page before that bookworm strangles you."

Gillian's gaze shot downward, and he jerked away from the book and fell off his chair. The worm flailed in the air, reaching blindly for the gnome. Sari pulled up her wand and directed it at the book. It slammed shut on the struggling worm.

"Damn worms have infested that book. There's no getting rid of them without compromising the integrity of the book's contents," Sari said.

"So don't go to sleep with this one open, huh?" Gillian said, righting himself and smoothing down his suit.

"One of your books tried to make me go cross-eyed," Reynolds said. "The print kept getting smaller and smaller and so I got closer to the page. When my nose was in it the blasted thing slammed shut, nearly taking it off."

Sari laughed merrily. "That will teach you to keep your nose out of romance books. I enchanted every one in the collection."

"Oh, well, I didn't realize I'd been set up," Reynolds replied. "And in my defense, I was looking for a line of poetry. It's been bugging me since I awoke from my statue state. There's a line from the great poet Anna Voy about waking up and being given a second chance at life and love. I can't recall it in its entirety, and you know how infuriating that can be."

"Fine, then," Sari said, flicking her wand at the library and muttering the reverse incantation for the spell. "Feel free to browse away, now."

"It's really an incredible collection of books, Sari," Reynolds said, looking at the shelves admiringly.

Sari, still pissed at Reynolds for his protectiveness, turned to Gillian. "Have you made any progress?"

He scratched his chin and stared at the oversized book with trepidation. "I'm not entirely sure what I'm looking for, since I haven't seen the page from the *Book of the Dead* yet."

"Oh, well, in that case." Sari pointed her wand at a bookcase on the far side of the room. A book bound in leather and tied closed with a blue ribbon flew across the room and landed in front of Gillian.

"What is this?" he asked.

"That's the *Book of Unknowing*," she answered. "It's for when you don't know what you're looking for. It can supply missing information, and the book changes based on who reads it. The complexity of the information it offers also changes, depending on the intelligence of the person reading it. I suspect it's just a picture book when Monet opens it."

Reynolds laughed at this. "That's funny, but I do hear that he's quite possibly the most brilliant potions maker Virgo has ever had—which would make him the greatest in Oriceran."

"Don't tell him that *ever*," Sari said. "I've worked his entire life to humble him and fix the imbalance that occurred when he was born on the night of the meteor shower." She bit her tongue, realizing she'd spoken directly to Reynolds when he was supposed to be receiving the quiet treatment.

Gillian gasped when he opened the book. "That's so strange. I was just thinking that I needed to brush up on my Egyptian mythology, and it's all here." He thumbed through the book, his eyes growing wide with shock.

"Then it's working," Sari said proudly.

"Is it all right if I borrow this?" Gillian asked, and stood, which put him in a significantly lower position than when he had been sitting in the chair.

Sari pretended to consider this with a great deal of reluctance, but after a moment she nodded. The truth was, there was no one more dependable than Gillian. Gnomes in general were known for their trustworthiness, but Sari had wanted to stress how important the book was.

"Thank you," Gillian said, pressing the book to his chest and scurrying toward the exit. "I have to speak with Finnegan about supplies for the Potions Shop before we leave."

"Tell him I said hello," Reynolds said, a teasing tone in his voice.

"Do *not* tell him that unless you want to instantly put him in a bad mood," Sari warned.

Gillian didn't seem to hear any of this as he hurried from the room. As soon as he was gone, Reynolds crossed the space between them and stood right in front of Sari.

She dropped her gaze to the floor. "I'd better be off to pack as well."

"Sari," Reynolds said, reaching for her hand. She pulled it away at once, admonishing him with a single look. How dare he be so forward when she was trying to hate him? "I'm sorry if my concern for your safety bothered you. I know how hard you have worked to convince yourself that I have no affection for you."

"Would you speak a language I understand? I swear, Reynolds, you've read too many poetry books lately," Sari snapped.

"Maybe I have." He snickered. "But my concern is founded. If you would simply allow an old wizard the chance to escort you, it would make me most grateful. I imagine I'd get no sleep if I stayed here and worried that something might have happened to you."

"Then you'd look even older and more tired than you do now," Sari said, turning away from the wizard and striding toward the bookcase in the corner.

"Well, if you wouldn't mind looking at me during this journey, I promise to make myself useful. I have a friend who has a herd of Pegasi. I'm sure he'll loan us three for the journey."

"You mean Almus, who illegally bred those animals?" Sari asked. "We've known for quite some time that he keeps them hidden in the north corner of Virgo."

Reynolds bowed his head slightly, a sheepish grin on his face. "Of course you're aware. Still, he owes me a favor, and would no doubt loan us the animals. They would make the journey quite easy."

Sari regarded Reynolds for a long moment, hoping her silence would make him squirm with uncertainty. "You mean that he owes you for smuggling him a supply of electric eels, and helping him sell brooms that supposedly fly?"

Reynolds lowered his chin, looking at the floor as his face reddened to match his goatee. "So you know about those things."

"Naturally," Sari said, scanning the shelves for the right book. "Honestly, making hardworking Virgoans think that a broom could fly. That's not a hard scam to get caught for."

"The enchantment wears off after an hour, which gives me enough time to make the sale," Reynolds said.

"If you were to put your efforts into doing good, then imagine the things you could accomplish."

"There really is a coven of witches who fly on brooms though, Sari," Reynolds said. "I've visited them in the East. They use a special type of wood that allows the brooms to fly. Enchantments always wear off eventually."

Sari had respected Reynolds when he was Azure's tutor. She had known he was often involved in illegal affairs, but she had turned a blind eye to it when she had been queen. For some reason she'd always had a soft spot when it came to the man before her. Often she thought it was his rebellious nature that had attracted her to him.

"I'd be very interested in seeing such a broom if you ever get a real one and not one that's a hoax," Sari said, pulling a book from the shelf. She flipped it open, almost at once finding the page she was looking for.

"I would never try to scam you," Reynolds said. "And it wouldn't work anyhow. You're too smart for me."

Sari pushed the volume into Reynolds' hands. "Here's the book you were looking for. You'll find this is the Anna Voy poem."

Reynolds looked down at the page, his mouth falling open as his eyes scanned the words. "You knew where to find it!"

"I know everything," she said, strolling off with a proud smile on her face.

3

The realtor's body lay on a long table in what used to be a science classroom in the old boarding school. Ata had found it to be the right spot for his potion-making spells.

Nenet eyed the body, disgust written on her face. "He's dead!" she said, walking around the body. It was pale, and rigor mortis was setting in.

"Yes. That's what happens when vampires drain all the blood from a person," Ata said, crushing up turmeric, which was a tasty spice and also the main ingredient in this spell. Curry spices were powerful when used in conjunction with other ingredients.

Nenet narrowed her green eyes at him and flashed her fangs menacingly. She wasn't going to attack him, because Cordelia had ordered all her vampires to leave Ata alone. Besides, she had just fed. He eyed the needle he'd used to withdraw his blood to feed Nenet. It wasn't an idea she'd warmed to originally, but they both knew she didn't want to attack people and distribute the virus. Those Nenet fed on would either die from blood loss or the virus that follower vampires spread with their bites.

"You're not the one who killed him, so I'm obviously not referring to you," Ata told her. Nenet was still so emotional about her change. It was wrong for him to think that they could interact as casually as they had when he was king.

"I can't believe you're going to send this monster after Queen Azure," Nenet said, picking up the stiff wrist of the dead realtor, then letting it fall.

"I don't have a choice," Ata said, gritting his teeth hard. He ground up the turmeric with a bit too much ferocity and turned it to powder instantly. That wouldn't do for this particular enchantment. He discarded it and grabbed another turmeric root.

"I completely understand," she said with a sensitive smile on her face. If anyone understood the mind control and torture Cordelia and Hamilton inflicted on their captives, it was Nenet. She pulled her hair over one shoulder, and as she absentmindedly braided it the gold bangles on her wrist clanged together, making music of a sort. Nenet had always played with her hair when stressed, needing to have her hands busy.

"I have no choice but to create this monster and send him after Azure," Ata said. "Strangely, I'm not even allowed to come up with a lesser solution. Their control requires me to put my best efforts into this one."

"I fear what will happen to Azure," Nenet told him.

"I know little of the queen, but I did sense that she was very capable when we met," Ata said, sprinkling the spices into the cauldron where it sparked. The liquid instantly turned orange.

He picked up a strand of blue hair and added it as well. They hadn't stayed long after Azure had knocked out everyone in the old hotel. However, the room where she'd been held had been searched, and Ata had found her blue hair. The controls Cordelia and Hamilton had placed on him caused him to serve diligently, so he had saved the hair just in case. It was this forethinking that made him the most powerful wizard in New Egypt, but now his ingenuity was being employed against the queen of Virgo.

"She did escape right under your nose," Nenet said.

"It's a good thing she did, because I've since figured out how to remove her necklace," Ata replied.

This produced a gasp from Nenet. "No!"

He nodded, remorse heavy in his gut. "Yes, and if I ever encounter the witch again, I'll have no choice but to use it on her."

"But then they'll turn her!"

"Which is why we have to hope she doesn't get caught again." Ata ladled the steaming liquid into a glass tube, which he held with a gripper to protect his hands. He gave Nenet a tentative look. "You will probably want to stand back for this."

She stepped back until she was against the wall, placing many of the old desks between her and the body. "I can't believe that you can perform this kind of magic. No wonder you were king."

Ata smiled slightly despite himself. He *was* powerful, and that was how he'd become king—by being the best. Ata missed his people. Surprisingly, he even missed his brother

Chibale. There was nothing his twin could do that he wouldn't forgive. And in truth, his brother hadn't known his actions would lead to all this. He hadn't known vampires were lurking, waiting to take over. Was it right for him to trick Ata so he could take the throne? No, but Chibale was notorious for fighting unfairly.

Ata parted the lips of the corpse and poured the potion into its mouth. The dead man wouldn't be burned by the temperature. The hot liquid would actually help wake up his body, and the potion ingredients would sustain him and tell him who to go after.

After all of the potion had been poured into the dead man's mouth, Ata stood back and waited for the transformation. Before their eyes all the color drained from the man's body, turning his skin a sickly gray, and his eyes sprang open, bloodshot and dark. A scream like glass breaking ripped from the monster's mouth. Nenet covered her ears; it seemed like the sound would never end. The man's mouth gaped, and the scream continued.

"Enough," Ata boomed.

The man froze and then began to thrash, smashing his arms and legs down hard on the surface beneath him.

"He's going to hurt himself," Nenet said, having to nearly shout over the racket to make herself heard.

Ata pointed his crook at the man before he rolled off the table and the monster threw his hands into the air, completely lost in his rampant emotions. He continued to scream as he threw himself across the table, as if trying to break his body.

Ata waved the crook in a figure eight and the dead man stopped, turned like a robot, and faced the wizard.

"You know who you are to go after?" Ata asked.

The man nodded, his eyes blank. He picked up the table in front of him as if suddenly overwhelmed by hot anger and threw it across the room, nearly hitting Nenet. As Ata had suspected, he was incredibly strong.

"You are to bring Azure back here. Do I make myself clear?" Ata asked.

Instead of answering, the monster grunted and flailed his arms over his head.

"How is he going to do that?" Nenet asked.

The man swiveled to face her with a crazed look in his eyes, then crouched and jerked his head back and forth like he was following an impossibly fast fly with his gaze.

"Shhh," Ata said, waving Nenet off. "No talking. He's disoriented, and could erupt."

As Ata finished speaking the man sprang up like a frog jumping and ran toward the desks, picking one up and throwing it straight at Nenet. She reacted immediately, using her enhanced speed to dart out of the way. She also shielded herself. The man already had picked up another desk to throw at her. It was like he was tossing pebbles rather than large pieces of furniture.

"Stop," Ata said, holding up a hand to the man. He froze, still holding another desk over his head. His dark eyes blinked at Ata, and then he looked blankly at Nenet. He let go of the desk, which smashed into the top of his head before sliding behind him to hit the floor. Unfazed, the monster grunted, spit flying from his mouth.

"No more," Ata commanded. "Now go." He pointed an authoritative finger at the exit.

The monster looked suddenly sad, as if he didn't want

to part from his creator. He dropped his chin and sluggishly moved around the desk toward the exit. Several times he looked longingly back at Ata, and after one final look he went out the door and disappeared.

Ata let out a heavy breath before facing Nenet. She didn't look scared, but she was definitely unnerved. "A zombie's bite makes its victim pass out," he said, answering her question from before.

"And once he bites her he can bring her back here?" Nenet said.

Ata nodded. "Where Cordelia and Hamilton will turn her."

They both stared at the door through which the zombie had exited, and a chill ran down Ata's spine. He'd used a forbidden spell, one his people had outlawed centuries ago, and there was a zombie prowling the streets of New Egypt because of him.

4

The baking heat of the desert diminished considerably when the group descended into the Sphinx. Since Laurel couldn't enter the structure due to her lack of magic, Manx and Finswick stayed back as well. They'd agreed to this arrangement too fast, which had instantly made Azure suspicious. However, she needed to leave for the Mountain of Truth soon, so she didn't stay to question the felines. Manx now took that form most of the time when he was with Laurel and Finswick.

"Just a bunch of cats hanging out on a fence," Manx had caroled at Azure's back as she left them.

Unlike the first time they had entered the Sphinx, this time the three didn't hesitate. They bustled through the false door that appeared to be a solid wall into the giant atrium. However, much like the first time they'd entered the New Egyptians' headquarters, most in the room had turned to stare at the blue-haired witch and her companions. Azure suspected they looked as strange to this clan as the New Egyptians did to her, with their tattoos and white robes. She stuck out like a sore thumb in her red robes. She had managed to conjure up a pair of jeans and a T-shirt for the upcoming journey, though. Gran was going to have a fit when Azure showed up wearing casual clothes. She grinned to herself, relishing the opportunity to be defiant.

The witches and wizards wading in the large fountain stole Azure's attention, but then she noticed something swaying at the back of the giant room. She started forward, but something held her back.

She gazed at the fingers wrapped around her arm. Ever was staring at the serpent that swayed behind the tall pillars as sunlight streamed onto it from overhead. Around the reptile were several witches and wizards, all of them kneeling with their heads bowed to the stone floor. The yellow snake was easily twenty feet tall, and its cobra-like head was four or five feet wide. A forked tongue flickered from its mouth as the snake hissed.

"That's dark magic," Ever said, his grip tightening on Azure's arm.

"I agree," Monet said, his face tense.

"Dark times call for dark measures," a voice called from the floor. Azure directed her attention to Cleo, who was Chibale's familiar. The sleek black cat was wearing the golden snake jewelry around its neck, just as she had when they first met her. Azure suddenly found it strange that Laurel and Finswick couldn't enter the Sphinx because they couldn't directly do magic, but Cleo could. There must have been an exception set up.

"Is that actually…" Azure pointed at the snake, which gave her chills even from this distance.

"Yes," Cleo answered, looking over her shoulder. "It's a wizard whom Chibale enchanted with shifting abilities." As Cleo spoke the serpent shrank and morphed into a man wearing the same robes as the rest. Also like them, his hands, arms, and legs were covered in tattoos.

"But that kind of shapeshifting would involve sacrifice," Monet stated, sounding offended. As well he should: it was a highly offensive topic, and a brand of magic that Virgo had outlawed long ago.

"Yes, and vampires are incredibly fearful of the cobra," Cleo stated matter-of-factly.

"Take us to the king," Azure demanded. "We have business to discuss with him."

Cleo eyed the queen, an entitled elegance in the cat's gaze. "Very well. Follow me," she finally said, strolling toward a nearby hallway.

They took the same path to the king's quarters as they had before and soon came to the round room where statues of the Egyptian god Anubis ringed the space. The figures were caryatids, and they held up the intricate crown molding that graced the room. The ceiling was a dome, and had been painted to look like a cloudy blue sky. In the middle of the room stood a throne covered in Egyptian hieroglyphs. On the throne, as if waiting for them, sat Chibale. His hands gripped the arms, and his eyes narrowed as Azure approached. She got the distinct impression that he was peeved about something.

Nefertiti stood on his right, her expression at first full of contempt. It began to shift as Azure drew closer.

"You found a tear," Chibale said, his tone disapproving.

So that was what this was about. The king had no idea.

He thought he could punish Azure for acting alone, but he was about to get his tattooed ass handed to him.

"I did," Azure said, halting a few feet from Chibale. Monet and Ever flanked her.

"And went through," Chibale said. "I believe the agreement was—"

"There was no agreement," Azure interrupted. "I was asked to find a tear. When I did, I went through it. It took me to the Sphinx on Earth."

Chibale nodded. "Naturally. They are portals between the sister cities."

"I found a page from the *Book of the Dead*," Azure said.

Disbelief jumped to Chibale's face. "You didn't! Hand it over."

Azure looked at Monet, and he gave a minute nod to reassure her. "I don't think so, King Chibale."

A deep line creased the space between Chibale's eyes and he gripped the lion's paws that terminated the arms of the throne. "How dare you? We have helped you. Given your friends refuge from the night. Who do you think you are, to deny us our ancient text?"

"I'm the one who can see the tears between New Egypt and Earth," Azure said calmly.

Cleo hissed loudly, looking up at Azure in defiance.

"Oh, quiet down, little kitty," Monet said, shaking his head at the cat.

"Your disobedience will be punished," Chibale said, withdrawing his flail from his robes. He swirled it and the dog-headed statues around the room came alive, moving their limbs robotically.

Ever and Monet whipped around to face the stone

guards headed toward them and Monet pointed his wand at the closest one, shooting a ray of blue light at it. The Anubis replica moved his staff down to intercept the ray. Ever was similarly defending against the statues thundering toward them.

Azure ignored them and stared coldly at Chibale. "How did you become king?"

His nostrils flared, and he shook his head roughly at her. "I'm the most powerful wizard in this coven. That's how queens and kings are chosen."

"But you are the most powerful wizard now only because you put a spell on Ata so he got lost in the desert," Azure accused.

"That is unacceptable. You can't make allegations about our king," Nefertiti said, but she didn't look offended so much as confused.

"These aren't allegations," Azure said. "These are facts. I was abducted by the vampires and brought back to New Egypt. It was there that I learned why the vampires have been so successful. They have a wizard working for them—against his will, of course."

Nefertiti spun to face Chibale. "This is so ridiculous. King Chibale, you shouldn't have to put up with this disrespect from an outsider."

Ever smashed one of the statues to dust beside Azure with a spell. Monet had bewitched one of them to do his bidding, and it turned on the others.

Chibale's mouth remained in a flat line. His eyes were dancing with fire, but there was nothing for him to say. Azure knew what only he and Ata had known: that Chibale had cursed his twin brother in order to steal his throne.

"Nefertiti, you shouldn't call him 'king' while the true one is enslaved," Azure said, her anger overwhelming her. She was an outsider in this affair, but because of that she was nonpartisan. She only wanted justice.

Nefertiti pulled her crook from her robes. "I'll make you pay for saying such a thing."

Azure reacted faster. She reached into her own robes and held Nenet's flail at the ready before Nefertiti could fire off a curse. The young witch froze, her large eyes pinned to the magical instrument in Azure's hand.

Ever had demolished all the Anubises on his side, but Monet was enjoying watching the two remaining statues wrestle. The one he had enchanted had the other in a headlock.

"I promise you that I have been with the vampires. It's because of Nenet that I was able to escape," Azure said, striding forward and handing the flail to the stunned witch. "She wanted you to have this. She said your crook will be more powerful if the two are together."

Nefertiti was incapable of speech for a moment. Her eyes welled with tears and her hand shook when she reached out and took the flail. "I never thought I'd feel the bond of our weapons again, but when you entered it returned. Ever so lightly, but still, it was there."

Azure nodded. "Yes, Nenet said the power you shared was diminished, but with her flail your crook would be stronger."

"You really saw her?" Nefertiti asked.

"Yes," Azure said, her eyes sliding to Chibale, who looked like the statues that had been stationed around the room with his expression frozen into quiet hostility. "I saw *both* your twins."

"You don't understand," he said through clenched teeth.

"Ata was really there?" Nefertiti asked. "He's not dead?"

Azure shook her head as Monet and Ever resumed their places beside her, having defeated all the statues. "He's alive, but he's the prisoner of two founder vampires, Cordelia and Hamilton.

"The ones who turned Nenet?" Nefertiti asked.

"That's right," Azure said. "And Ata is powerless. He's their magical slave, forced to do all that they ask."

Nefertiti whipped around to face Chibale. "Did you do what she said? Did you curse Ata?"

Chibale looked down at Cleo, who was perched beside his throne, and then at the broken statues. "You wouldn't understand, Nefertiti. The throne has been fought over for centuries. Ata knew his time would come, just as mine will one day. Holding this position means you must always be on high alert, and he let his guard down. The supreme king doesn't allow himself to be cursed or overthrown."

Nefertiti's hands vibrated as she threw them overhead, crook and flail clutched tightly. "Ata would never have done something like this to you. He took the throne when your father passed. Even though he could have proven his power before, he waited until your father, our king, had died. You are a cruel, cruel man, Chibale."

Nefertiti, eyes full of tears, sped from the room, her feet urgently kicking off the stone.

"I hope you're happy now," Chibale said, his tone cool and lifeless.

"You got yourself into this mess on your own," Monet said, adding his bit to the conversation.

"None of you can understand the sacrifices I've had to make," Chibale said. "That is the way of the New Egyptians. Ata was not willing to be proactive in defending our people, so I did what was best for our coven."

"You did what was best for your ego," Ever said, with a tone in his voice that made Azure proud.

"And now you're using sacrificial spells," Azure said. "I'm fairly certain that the council will not approve."

Chibale jumped off the throne, his eyes bursting with anger. "The council members don't have vampires strolling the streets of their villages."

"If you had informed the council they could have helped," Azure said.

"They'd have quarantined us, and you know it," Chibale said. "No one would be able to enter or exit New Egypt. It would be our end."

"You don't know that, because you've stuck your head in the sand and deluded yourself into thinking that betraying your brother and using illegal practices is warranted," Azure said. She pointed to herself. "But know this, Chibale: no matter what you do, I won't turn my back on you. My cabinet isn't going to desert you." She gestured to Monet and Ever.

Chibale seemed to shrink a little, and his shoulders sagged. "I don't see why not. Who *wouldn't* run from this? We're a cursed land with vampirism spreading across it, and since they have Ata, we have no chance of defeating them."

"If you give up, New Egypt is doomed," Azure said. "I

can help, but if you as king stop leading your people then they will fall victim to these monsters."

"I'm not the king, and you know it," Chibale said, having shifted in demeanor considerably. He had been deluding himself with untruths, but being confronted with his brother's abduction was making him wake up.

"You are not the true king, Chibale," Azure agreed, "but right now you're all this coven has. Lead them and protect them as your brother would."

Azure, realizing it was getting late and they needed to get on the road soon, turned for the exit. She'd done what she'd come for.

"Where are you going? What are you going to do?" Chibale asked.

Azure turned back, allowing a small excited smile to show. "I'm going to try to stop the vampires."

"How?" Chibale asked, taking a step in her direction, his eyes brimming with remorse.

"Do you think you can decipher the page from the *Book of the Dead*?" she asked.

He shook his head. "Not quickly, we can't. It took ages to decode the book."

"I figured as much. I'm taking the page to a gnome who might be able to help," Azure said, clearing her throat. "I'm also seeking the counsel of the great Mage Lenore, and I'm going to try and secure the bat population in Lancothy before the founders do."

"'Cause that's how we roll. Overachievers, we are," Monet said.

Chibale stared around the destroyed room and then back at Azure. "You and your cabinet are very skilled and brave, and New Egypt will owe you a great debt when this is all over. I'll ensure that the king remembers to pay that debt."

"But first we must free him," Azure reminded him, and left.

5

"And then I was like, hey, quit hitting yourself. *Quit hitting yourself.*" Monet laughed, explaining how he'd made the statue knock itself in the face. "Then I had the statue I was controlling give the other one a wet willy. I think the idea was lost on those dry pieces of rock, though."

Ever laughed. "Yeah, let's hope we didn't just destroy ancient artifacts."

The three were strolling down the road next to their hotel, where the carriage was presently parked. The cobbled streets were thick with people, most hoping to get their shopping done before nightfall.

The vampire epidemic was now common knowledge. Many of the carts they passed were selling pouches of lizard ashes, hawk feathers fashioned into talismans, and falcon claws, which were items supposed to repel bats and vampires. All of them were hoaxes, meant solely to make innocent people shell out their money.

Many of the passersby had owls in cages, purchases they'd made hoping the animals would kill any bats that approached them before they melded with their magic.

"This is scary," Azure said. She paused in the middle of the lane and watched the subtle cues of chaos breaking out around the city as the residents' fear mounted higher.

Ever rubbed his hands on his jeans and nodded in agreement. He moved closer to Azure, constantly scanning the crowd.

"Yeah, that paisley shawl totally doesn't match that woman's ugly argyle socks," Monet said, pointing at an old woman who was hobbling through the crowd. "Seriously, argyle and paisley? What was that witch thinking?"

Azure followed his finger and a jolt hit her in the chest. She recognized that woman! Was it possible?

"Come on," Azure said, bolting forward. "We have to follow her."

"I don't think her wardrobe warrants an intervention. I was just saying it was an eyesore," Monet said.

Azure pushed through the crowd, trying to keep her eyes on the shawl as it moved away. "That's the woman who gave me this necklace."

The woman was about to bump into a brick wall. Azure, with Ever and Monet on her heels, picked up speed, bumping hard into people as she traversed the crowd. Most were headed in the opposite direction, which slowed their progress.

Suddenly the brick wall shifted, and a canopy sprouted over a door. The sign above the shop read **Myrtle's Collectibles**. The old woman pushed through the door and was gone. They were only five yards away, but the door was disappearing like it had done the first time. Azure slammed hard into a tall wizard and pushed to get around him.

"Excuse me. Sorry. Coming through," she said, feeling awful for her impoliteness.

"She's so damn pushy," Monet said behind her, and laughed.

The shop was just ahead, but was quickly fading. The canopy had all but disappeared, and the sign now read *My le s Co ect es*.

"Come on!" Azure yelled and dove for the door handle. She had her fingers on it just as it disappeared completely but she still felt the warm metal in her hands, so she pushed down on the handle and swung the door open.

The old witch spun around when the bell chimed over the door. She'd just lowered the shawl to reveal her black hair, which was streaked with gray. Her black eyes stared at the three with stubborn petulance as they clambered into the shop.

"We're closed," the woman said, bustling around the counter.

Ignoring the woman, Azure strode to the glass counter. It was filled with odd trinkets and potion bottles, and there was a case on the wall that held shrunken gnome heads. Azure was immediately grateful that Gillian wasn't with them now.

"You're the one who gave me this necklace." She held up the ruby in her fingers for the woman to see.

Myrtle squinted at the necklace and pursed her lips. "You have me confused with someone else. My face is like that—easy to confuse with others."

The old witch had said that before, but there was no way she could be mixed up with someone else. Her tattoos ended at the base of her chin, but spread over her neck and chest and arms.

"I just want to know why you gave me the necklace. Was there a specific reason?" Azure pressed.

The woman pulled a lizard from her robes and set him in a small box lined with velvet. "I realize I can't trick her, thank you very much. It was worth a try," she said to the lizard before looking up at Azure. "Technically I didn't give it to you. I just handed it off to you."

"It came from Mage Lenore, though, right?" Azure insisted. "She's your cousin, you said."

Mage Lenore looked nothing like this woman. Maybe they were distant cousins twice-removed.

"Hey, Az, check this out," Monet said from the other side of the shop. He had a silver lamp in his hands that was very similar to the one she'd found.

"What have I told you about touching things when we're in public?" Azure admonished, striding over to him.

"So you don't think I should lick it then?" Monet asked, sticking out his tongue and holding the lamp dangerously close to his mouth.

"I use a polish that is poisonous, and there is no anti-dotal potion. Go ahead," Myrtle encouraged matter-of-factly.

"I'm good. I know the Potions Master from Virgo. He's sublimely talented," Monet said.

"That's funny," Myrtle said, not laughing. "I heard he was dead. Something about not being able to keep his mouth shut."

"Ha-ha, crazy old woman," Monet said, closing one eye and peering into the spout of the lamp. "You think there's a genie in here? Maybe you should rub it, and then you'll have two genies."

"I'm certain it's not the same—"

"Did you just say *two* genies?" The old witch was suddenly right next to Azure, head even with her shoulder. Azure looked down at the woman, trying to find room to step away from her in the cramped store.

"Weren't you just over there?" Monet asked.

"Hogwash," the woman said, waving him off and turning to Azure. "Do you have a genie's lamp?"

Azure felt quite sandwiched, with the witch nearly on top of her and Ever at her back. He'd hurried over as soon as the witch had appeared out of thin air.

"I do," she said and reached into her robes, pulling out the lamp she carried with her everywhere for security reasons.

"Is there a genie in there?" the witch asked. She shot her eyes to the counter where the lizard sat. "I'm well aware of what she's going to say, but I need her to say it."

"Uhhhh… Yes, there's a genie in my lamp." Azure turned the lamp around and whispered into the spout, "Can you join us out here, Bob?"

From the lamp a booming voice called, "I'm in the shower, so no."

"Bob, when I ask for your presence you're to obey," Azure said.

"Is that a wish you're making?" Bob asked. "Because you only have one left before I don't have to look at your ugly face anymore."

Azure lowered the lamp and looked at the witch. "Bob is a bit of a special genie. We're working on his murderous tendencies and verbal abuse."

"Can you really blame him?" Myrtle asked. "All genies are like that. They are enslaved beings who suffer imprisonment and isolation." The witch spun around and threw up her hand, and the box where the lizard sat flipped upside down so that the lizard was now trapped under the box. "That's nothing like my situation. You mind your tongue!"

"Is he okay?" Monet asked, pointing to the upside-down box. A second later the lizard's head peeked out from under the box.

"I'm fine," he chirped. "It's a game Myrtle and I play. I spout truths, and she retaliates with anger and verbal abuse —about like the genie."

"A talking lizard," Monet said, sliding his eyes to Azure. "That's totally normal."

"You speak to a cat every day," she said.

"I would prefer *not* to speak to the cat, but when I ignore him he pees in my shoes," Monet said.

Azure shook her head, giggling about Monet's ongoing battle with Finswick. She held the lamp up again and said, "Bob, will you please join us out here?"

"If this isn't an emergency, I'd prefer not to. I'm in the middle of reading a book about an assassin. He's just about to kill his boss, and—"

"Bob!" Azure yelled into the spout.

The smoke shot straight out of the spout toward the ceiling. When Bob appeared his hands were over his ears, making his bushy armpits visible. As usual he was shirtless, but covered in hair. The bristling mustache he sported covered his expression well. "You didn't have to yell. That echoes horribly in there." He shook his head as if his ears were ringing.

"I was under the impression that you had to follow my direct orders," Azure said.

Bob floated up and down, both his arms and legs crossed. "In the Genie Bylaws it's more of a guideline. We can chalk up most of our insubordination to bad hearing, miscommunications or Insta being in retrograde. That damn planet will screw up a whole host of conversations, so I usually take those days off."

"He's amazing," Myrtle said, staring wide-eyed at the genie.

"He's a pain in the ass," Monet said, picking up another genie-type lamp that sat on the shelf.

"And there's nothing wrong with your hearing," Ever said, resting his hands on his hips.

"Huh? What did you say?" Bob asked.

"So these lamps here…they don't have genies in them?" Azure asked Myrtle.

"Oh, no. I received them after the genie had long been liberated," Myrtle said.

"Liberated?" Azure and Bob repeated in unison.

"Jinx." Monet laughed.

Azure waved him off and opened her mouth to speak, but nothing came out.

"Yes, dear Azure, that's how jinxes work," Monet said, looking satisfied.

Bob's mouth was moving quickly, but there was no sound there either.

"Oh, peace! It has finally arrived." Monet sighed.

Ever laughed, but quickly covered it after receiving a scornful look from Azure. "Why don't you let this one go and jinx Azure later. Maybe when she's sleeping, so she doesn't wake us all up snoring."

Azure's lips popped open and she mouthed the words, "I don't either."

"Sure you don't, and it isn't so loud that you wake us up on the other side of the carriage," Ever teased.

"That's Finswick, if I'm being honest," Monet said. "But yes, I'll withdraw my jinx just this once. Azure Azure Azure. Bob Bob Bob."

Bob, who hadn't stopped talking since being jinxed, said, "Simultaneously, I'll have these pirates called the 'Kezza' or 'Kazza' or something like that pillage the carriage so that your murder won't be connected to me. And then..." The genie's voice trailed away when he realized that he was speaking aloud and all eyes were on him.

"Wow, you're one fucked-up genie," Monet said.

"Premeditation makes the sentence worse by council law," Ever said.

Bob's head sank and he pretended to snore loudly, as if he had instantly fallen asleep.

Azure looked around. "Where did Myrtle go?" The old witch had been claustrophobically close, but now she was gone.

Monet made his way over to the counter. He lifted the

box to find the lizard still there, curled up and sleeping. The reptile opened one eye and peered up at the wizard.

"Where did the crazy old witch go?" Monet asked.

"She prefers to be called 'eccentric,'" the lizard said, yawning. "She's in the back. Myrtle likes to disappear."

"Crazy and eccentric old witch, where are you?" Monet called.

Azure joined Monet at the counter as the witch appeared on the other side. "Is that the disappearing and reappearing trick you use?" she asked Monet.

Myrtle's left eye twitched, making her cheek jerk strangely. "He can't do this."

"But I've seen him do it," Azure said.

"As have I," Ever said, beside them now.

The old witch shook her head. "No, only those with House of Torrance lineage can disappear and relocate."

Azure turned slowly, giving Monet a stunned look. His face accurately reflected his disbelief. "Is there something you want to tell me, Monet Torrance?"

He gulped. "I don't know anything. You know that."

"You're a Torrance? But you come from Virgo!" Myrtle exclaimed.

"My mother was from Virgo. She brought me there after my father's disappearance. Can you tell me anything about him?" Monet's question came at lightning speed. He'd always been curious about his father, Azure knew, but he also wasn't one to dwell. And after his mother died, he'd had enough to deal with.

Myrtle shook her head roughly before jerking her eyes down to where the lizard sat. "Silence, or you'll find your-self in my stew tonight."

"Please, if you know something about Monet's fath—"

"I don't know anything," the witch said and then cleared her throat. "I'm guessing that you want to know how to liberate your genie."

"Finally we're talking about something important," Bob said, swirling through the air to land right next to the witch, who was clearly hiding something. "Go on, then. Tell me how I can be freed. Do I have to gut my master? Behead her? Poison her? I'm prepared to do whatever it takes."

"Shut up, Bob, or I won't help you," Azure said.

"That's not true," Bob said. "You're a good witch, and do impractical things all the time to help others. It's a real shortcoming."

Azure rolled her eyes. "Myrtle, will you please just tell us how to free Bob? He's a real pain in the ass, and I can't imagine punishing another with his service."

The witch stared down at the lizard, probably having a silent conversation with him. She finally nodded and said, "Yes, I'll tell you how to free the genie, but first you have to do something for me."

"Of course," Monet said, throwing his hands into the air.

"You are going to Lancothy, and there you will find—"

"How did you know that?" Ever asked, cutting her off.

The witch regarded the Light Elf with an impatient stare before saying, "If you bring me back a scale from a weredragon, I will tell you how to free Zingamobobfren."

"Zingamobobfren?" Azure asked, nearly laughing. "That's your full name, Bob?"

The genie cradled his head in hands, gripping his turban. "No! Now they know and will make fun of me."

"'Zingamobobfren' is a much better name than 'Bob' for a genie," Ever said.

"I agree. I think I'll call you 'Zingy,'" Monet said.

"My name is *Bob*," the genie said. His face was red when he looked up from his hands.

"Okay, Myrtle, we'll bring you a weredragon's scale," Azure said, thinking she'd just signed up for an impossible task. How was she going to do that?

The witch regarded the crystal ball on the counter and shook her head. "The odds are against you, but give it your best shot. It's important that you don't use your last remaining wish, or Zingamobobfren will move on and your chance to free him will be lost."

"Okay, don't use the wish. Got it," Azure said, turning to look out the shop window. They needed to get going.

"Oh, and one more thing..." Myrtle said.

"Let me guess. We're all going to die?" Monet asked, singing the question a bit.

Myrtle shook her head. "No. I'm pretty sure that you, Monet Torrance, go on to invent the elixir of life." She turned her dark eyes on Azure and grabbed her hand. The woman's bony fingers were icy cold and hard, but Azure didn't pull away. "Tell my dear cousin she's chosen well."

6

Obviously Azure wanted to know what Myrtle had meant when she said that Mage Lenore had chosen well, but the crazy-ass witch disappeared and they all felt pushed to the exit. As soon as they opened the door they were tossed into the street by an invisible force, and Myrtle's Collectibles disappeared.

Azure found herself pacing back and forth in the carriage as it rode through the streets of New Egypt. How was she going to get a dragon scale? Was it worth potentially offending a weredragon to free Bob? He was an ungrateful asswit who got her in more trouble than he prevented. Well, besides helping her escape from the vampires—but he had also almost gotten her caught.

Getting a scale from a weredragon would be difficult or Myrtle would have just gotten it herself, Azure assumed. There were so many questions running through her mind, like Monet's...

He was on the other side of the carriage teaching Laurel

how to play the card game Elements. Someone should probably warn the werecat that Monet cheated, and she was probably going to get soaking wet or scorched. Azure smiled a little when she spied Manx in raven form sitting on the sideboard, peeping at Monet's cards from behind his back. The pooka flapped his wings and flew up, and when he was over the table he landed and changed into a bunny, then hopped over and settled down next to Laurel's elbow. The whole lot were just a bunch of cheaters.

Azure stumbled when the carriage took flight and fell hard into Ever, who was standing next to the grand piano. He caught her and kept her from falling to the floor and she secured her balance by holding onto the piano, but it was a challenge while the carriage was gaining speed and elevation.

"Hold on," Ever said, gripping her shoulders tightly. "You know, you really should sit down for a takeoff, unless you're a flight attendant and used to sudden altitude changes."

Azure pressed her back into the piano and looked up at Ever in confusion. "What's a 'flight attendant?'"

He smiled at her ignorance. "I'll take you on a plane ride on Earth sometime and show you firsthand."

"You keep promising to take me on all these adventures on Earth. When are we going to have the time?" she asked.

His face was full of amusement. "I assume we'll have time. I plan on living a long time and I'm guessing that my life will be spent protecting yours, so you can join me on all the adventures."

Azure choked on a sip of air, now realizing how close Ever was to her. Since the embrace the night she'd escaped from Cordelia and Hamilton she'd been much more sensitive to their dynamic, which had shifted—or maybe her understanding had. She didn't look at Ever the same way she looked at Monet, and he didn't look at her as a friend either. There was longing in Ever's stare, a strange poetic look that she'd never seen when anyone looked at her. Most had reverence for her as queen, but this was different. This was something she didn't understand.

The carriage leveled out and Azure worked her jaw back and forth to pop her ears. Flying definitely took some getting used to. Feeling unbalanced, she found herself pushing away from Ever, but realized that there was nowhere to go with the giant piano at her back. Wait, where had it come from?

"Has this piano always been here?" Azure asked, turning to face the sleek black instrument. She ran her hand over the top, enjoying its smoothness.

Ever shook his head. "Oak added it when he created yours and Laurel's bedroom. He said that the guys didn't deserve their own sleeping quarters, but we could have something that made us more refined."

Azure laughed. "He's trying to culture you to subdue your boyish ways."

Ever joined in, laughing too. "What's strange is that I play the piano. I have since I was a child."

"Why is that strange?" Azure asked.

"Because when I proudly informed Oak that I was refined enough to know how to play Frederic Chopin's Scherzo Number 2 Opus 31, he nodded and said he was well aware."

"He's a very interesting man," Azure mused, thinking of

the strange carriage. Then, as if her memory was finally catching up with her, she turned abruptly to Ever. "Did you say you play the piano? Is this Chopin piece from Earth?"

Ever nodded, a lopsided grin on his face. It produced a small dimple on his left cheek which she'd never noticed before. "It's one of the most famous pieces, and if I do say so myself, incredibly challenging to play."

"Well then, I must hear it," Azure said, pushing him toward the piano bench. He pushed back into her, not taking the seat.

"I'm not so sure I'm in the mood to play that just now," he said, and motioned to the bench. "Why don't you take a seat and I'll teach you some things?"

Azure had never learned to play a musical instrument. Her hours had been spent in art, history, literature, and practical magic lessons. Her mother had always said that a queen must know where they'd been in order to know where to lead the people, so her education had heavily involved history and learning the laws of the kingdom.

She shrugged and remained standing. "I'm not really the musical type."

Ever frowned and tapped a few of the keys, his fingers gliding across them effortlessly. "Oh, that's not true. We're all musical. You just have to know the notes to play."

He rhythmically ran his fingers over the white and black keys, producing a beautiful melody.

"Keep that racket down," yelled Monet. "I'm trying to hear these two, since they are whispering." He swept his hand toward Laurel and Manx. The cats had stayed back while they went into the Sphinx, and seemed to have achieved a bonding of sorts.

Ever pulled his hand from the piano with a playful grin on his face. "Maybe another time, then," he said to Azure.

"If I catch you two cheating I'll have the queen behead you," Monet threatened.

"What do you make of the Torrance business?" Azure asked, gazing across the room at Monet.

Ever glanced over his shoulder briefly before turning back around. "I'm not certain. I suppose he's related to a powerful lineage of witches and wizards. Maybe even Mage Lenore, since she's cousin to Myrtle."

Azure sighed. "I wonder if the old witch will tell us anything?"

"Perhaps," Ever said, his eyes low. He was clearly thinking.

"'Perhaps.'" Azure repeated his word with a different inflection. "I like that word. 'Perhaps.'" She smiled inwardly.

"It does have a nice sound," Ever agreed.

"I like words. The sounds they make, and the things they mean," Azure said.

"'That only led to a lonely life accompanied by the last words of the already dead, so I came here looking for a Great Perhaps, for real friends and a more-than-minor life,'" Ever recited from memory.

"That's a beautiful string of words," she said, liking everything about that sentence.

"It was written by an author on Earth named John Green. He writes like we breathe," Ever said.

"Effortlessly?" Azure guessed.

Ever nodded. "Yes, and with a rhythm to keep your heart beating."

Azure felt she'd just fallen into a conversation that she never wanted to end. It, like the words of this John Green, was effortless, and just as fulfilling as breathing. "I had no idea you were a renaissance man who played the piano and was well versed in Earth literature."

Ever leaned in and spoke from the corner of his mouth. "I'm also well versed on literature from Oriceran, but I don't mean to brag."

Azure reached out and playfully slapped his arm. "You do too."

Finswick jumped onto the surface of the piano and strolled over to them. "I hope I'm interrupting. I have an idea for you."

Azure slid her gaze to her black and white familiar, who was licking his paw and looking at her with his usual calm superiority. "I'm all ears."

"Bob told me you have to find a scale from a weredragon," Finswick began.

"Yes. I guess I'm going to have to ask one in Lancothy. Laurel said that there is an ancient family of them there," Azure said.

"Then she probably also informed you that they'll scorch your hair off for such a request," Finswick said, lowering his paw.

"Yes, she said it was pretty much like someone asking me to shave a section of my head," Azure said, feeling the doubt creep back over her thoughts.

"And while you might look all right with a shaved head, I don't think it's worth being torched to secure Bob's freedom," Finswick said.

From the lamp on the side table Bob spilled out into the

room. "If the queen wants to endanger her life to save mine, that's her business."

Finswick resumed cleaning himself with his paw. "You could use your last wish to ask for the protection of Virgo from threats and be done with this buffoon."

"Who you calling a monkey?" Bob asked, brandishing a fist at the cat.

"'Buffoon,' not 'baboon,'" Finswick corrected.

"Oh, well, I don't get out much," Bob said, throwing his hand in Azure's direction. "I blame her. She never takes me anywhere and she never lets me do anything. She ruined my life."

Azure thought of reminding Bob that she hadn't even known him very long, but what was the point? She rolled her eyes, catching the grin on Ever's face.

"Can I just say my life has gotten very colorful since meeting you and your cast of characters?" Ever said.

"You're one of these circus freaks, so just keep that in mind," Azure responded.

"And per Section Twelve, Sub-point Q of the Genie Bylaws, I'm unable to offer forever protection to a land," Bob said matter-of-factly.

"Useless," Finswick said. "He's absolutely useless."

Azure shook her head. "He *has* helped. And regardless, no one deserves to be trapped in a lamp all their life."

"Which feels endless," Bob complained, pretending to sob into his hands.

"You are immortal, so…" Ever said.

Finswick brought her back to the subject at hand. "Anyway, if you won't listen to reason, then I have a solution for you."

"Yes, what is it?" Azure asked.

"Oak appears to have a way with dragons. Have you thought about asking him for help?" Finswick asked.

Azure tilted her head to the side. She hadn't thought to ask Oak, but he did have four tame dragons. It was reasonable that he might know how to get a weredragon scale.

"You're a genius, Finswick!" Azure said, grabbing the cat and giving him a hug.

"I'm the one who told the cat about my dilemma, because I knew there had to be a good solution," Bob said, now blowing his nose on a handkerchief he'd grabbed from nowhere.

Azure lifted her head from Finswick's fur. "You're a genius too, Bob."

"Genius." Bob coughed. "The Genius Genie. I like the sound of that. I'm changing my name."

"Oh, hell no you're not, Zingamobobfren," yelled Monet from across the room.

7

The carriage began to descend an hour later. When they landed in a grassy clearing surrounded by lush trees and sprinkled with lavender, Oak informed the parties in the carriage that the dragons needed to rest before continuing the trek.

"Flying to the Mountain of Truth is an exhausting trip for them because of the magic they have to break through," he told Azure when she exited the carriage into the bright sunlight outside.

"They *will* be able to find Mage Lenore's house, won't they?" Azure asked.

Oak pulled his pointy hat off his head, pushing his bluish-silver hair out of his face. He looked like an old wizard with his long beard, but his eyes were full of youthful energy. "You've been to Mage Lenore's house, isn't that right?"

Azure nodded as the rest of the group filed out of the

carriage to stretch their legs. Manx flew to the tree line in raven form. "Don't go too far," Azure called.

"I'm just going to catch a mouse for supper," the pooka told her, and disappeared.

Azure shivered in disgust.

"Yes, mademoiselle," Oak stated, withdrawing a pipe from his robe and lighting it with the tip of his knobby wand. "All one needs is to have visited Mage Lenore's house once to be able to return, I do believe. I've never been there myself, but you have. That should be enough."

"That must be how Gran is getting there. She's going with Gillian, who was with me," Azure mused.

"Your gran is an incredible woman who could get to Mage Lenore's all on her own," Oak said, puffing on the pipe.

Azure smiled. Gran was by far the most incredible person she'd ever known, but she couldn't tell the old woman that. She'd probably barf at the sentiment.

"Oak, I have a question for you." Azure stared at the Baltic Long-tooth dragons, which were stretched out in different places, fast asleep. Micky, the dragon who had defended Monet and Ever against Cordelia, lay closest, her spikey tail thumping the ground loudly.

"Your tone suggests that you're riddled with uncertainty regarding this question," Oak said, raising an eyebrow at her.

"Well, I need something in order to free Bob from the lamp, but I don't know how to get it," Azure said. She wasn't sure why she didn't just ask him directly, but it felt like a conversation that deserved a bit of lead-up.

Oak held out his hand. "Do you mind if we walk, mademoiselle? The dragons need to rest, and I need to exercise. We tend to need opposites. Such is the relationship of dragons and their master."

Azure nodded, since she wanted a chance to walk in nature as well. Being in New Egypt was nice, but she missed trees and plants. They strolled through the clearing, the long grass caressing Azure's robe. "My question is actually regarding dragons."

"Yes, I figured as much." Oak blew out a cloud of purple smoke. "Most come to me for my knowledge of dragons, but don't underestimate this old wizard. I have been able to tame the legendary creatures because I've mastered many other things."

"I think that makes sense. You appear to be an incredibly wise wizard."

He turned to face her with a spark in his bluish-silver eyes. "Wisdom is one thing, but a wise man can still be a fool. I've mastered my own heart, which is one reason I'm talented enough to tame the dragons. These wickedly wonderful creatures trust me because I have proved myself to be true. It is a pure man who can tame a beast. It is the one who knows himself who can master others."

Azure didn't know what to say to this. It sounded as though her education wouldn't offer her anything unless she knew who she truly was. That was a strange concept for her to contemplate as such a young witch.

"Of course, it all takes time," Oak said, seemingly hearing her thoughts. "We cannot know our own heart without the experiences to learn its music."

Azure continued walking. For some reason the mention of music and hearts startled something deep in her bones.

"Now, you have a question for me. Please, no pretenses, mademoiselle," Oak said, striding next to her. The sun was shining overhead, but was quickly making its descent. Azure enjoyed the glow it sprinkled onto the grass and treetops.

Azure explained what Myrtle needed to help her free Bob. When she was done, Oak took a long pull on his pipe, his eyes focused on nothing.

"You're right to be hesitant with your question," Oak began. "You are a powerful and lovely queen, respected for your bravery as well as your compassion, but you stand no chance at all of securing a scale from a weredragon. It's just not something they would offer to a person like you."

"Because I'm not one of them?" Azure asked.

Oak thought on this for a moment, then shook his head. "No, it's not a matter of being like them, but rather of relating to them. Could you imagine being neither human nor a dragon, being something in-between?"

Azure shook her head. "I could not, but I can't imagine what it's like to be a genie either and yet I don't think enslaving them is right. Empathy may not be my strong suit, but every day I must make choices for my people that are in their best interests. I can't always relate to them, so I have to do what I feel is right in my own heart."

Oak smiled, and Azure realized how handsome he was. Under the beard he had a face with all the right angles. "I think you're well on your way to mastering your own heart, talking like that."

"But it doesn't matter. The weredragons won't give me a scale, will they?" Azure asked.

"I'm afraid they will not," Oak said. "They would, however, give one to me."

Azure halted, turning at once to the old wizard. "They would? That would be great!"

Oak held up his long-fingered hand. "Please contain yourself, mademoiselle. Although I will get a weredragon's scale when we're in Lancothy, I cannot give it to you."

"What?" Azure asked, unsure if she had misheard Oak. "You won't give it to me?"

"I won't give it to you without receiving something in return," Oak said.

"Oh, well, that's fair," Azure said, hiccupping in her excitement. There was hope after all. "I can pay you whatever you want."

"Anyone could pay me," Oak began. "I want something from you that you're in a unique position to give. It's incredibly powerful, and would benefit me a great deal."

"Okay, do you want to give me a riddle like most, or will you simply tell me what you want?" Azure asked teasingly.

Oak smiled in return, that elegant handsomeness radiating from his features again. "Of course. What I want from you won't be easy to obtain. It's an emotion. A unique feeling."

"What you want me to give you is an emotion?"

Oak nodded. "But I want you to bottle this emotion, in a way, although that's not really possible. First you must figure out how to contain it, since it tends to be intangible. I've heard of a binding spell that when cast can contain certain emotions so their magic can be used."

"Do you mean like when we're happy? There's a way to

'bottle' that so it can be reused?" Azure asked, using air quotes.

"Happiness is a very strong emotion, and if it was used in a potion or a spell it would have profound effects."

This made sense to Azure. "So I need to first figure out how to contain an emotion for magical repurposing, is that right?"

"Correct," Oak said. "But unfortunately this isn't like potions work."

So Monet wouldn't be able to help her. This was getting more complicated by the minute.

"All right, I'll figure it out. Someone has to know how to contain an emotion," Azure said.

"Certainly someone does, but you must find the right person for this emotion since it's rare and quite fragile," Oak told her.

Azure stopped walking again, her face creasing with worry. "What emotion are you asking me to find and contain?"

"Only one of the most incredible man has ever known. Mademoiselle, you must deliver me the emotion tied to true love."

8

"Hold on tight. It's going to be a bumpy ride the rest of the way," Oak said, closing the door behind Azure. She stared at the wizard, watching him watch her through the window. She wasn't sure why, but she constantly got the impression that he was more than he seemed. Finally she heeded his warning and took a seat at the couch.

"Is Oak going to help you?" Ever asked as he sat down in the armchair next to her.

"Yeah. He's going to get me the dragon scale, but in return I must give him something impossible," Azure stated, suddenly feeling sorry for herself—an emotion she wasn't good at. She heard Gran's words in her head: "We all have problems. No one has that market cornered."

"If the curious look on my face isn't accurately communicating it, you've got my attention," Ever said.

Azure tried to smile, but it didn't really reach her eyes. "He wants true love."

"Wow, talk about mixing business with pleasure," Monet said, taking a seat on the couch, placing his bare feet next to Azure, and poking her with his toes. "Not to mention that he's like a billion years older than you."

Azure sniffed, inching away from Monet's feet. "Not from me. He just wants me to bottle the emotion of true love and give it to him. Then Myrtle gets what she wants, and Bob gets his freedom."

"Well, to do that you're going to—"

"Have to figure out how to contain an emotion with a spell," Azure cut Ever off. She was irritable, and it was starting to bug her.

"Well, yeah, but I meant that you'll have to find true love," Ever said

Azure pulled her gaze from Ever's, feeling exceptionally uncomfortable.

"That's easy. Once you have the containing spell, you can just use it when I open a bottle of centaur vodka," Monet said. He lifted a bottle from the floor and uncorked it, then pressed the bottle to his mouth and took a long sip. "Ahhh, true love." Monet wiped his hand over his wet lips.

Azure held out her hand. "I don't think I have the same attraction to this stuff, but go ahead and share."

Monet held it close to his chest before relinquishing it. "I'm running low. I only have a case left."

Azure nearly spit out her drink. "You're down to a case? What, do you bathe in this stuff?"

"Hell no." Monet scoffed at her. "That would be disgusting. Now, ranch dressing...I'd totally take a bath in that. Mmmmm, with fries and pizza." He looked at the ceiling dreamily, as if picturing himself taking a ranch bath while gorging on greasy food.

The carriage lurched to the side and Azure nearly fell forward. Luckily—and grossly—Monet's foot caught her. She gripped the side of the couch before the next lurch tossed her up to the ceiling.

"Hey, don't spill the stuff," Monet said, pointing to the bottle bobbing in Azure's hands. Centaur vodka came up out of the top and dripped over her hand, and she pressed it to her mouth to preserve it. Another jolt made a large dollop splash into her mouth. Monet pulled the bottle away from her, looking concerned that she was going to drown in his vodka, and also that she was going to drink it all.

Purple-pinkish smoke blanketed the carriage suddenly and Laurel, who had sunk her claws into the couch opposite them, stared out the windows in alarm. "Is this normal?"

"I've never flown here, but I think so," Azure said, her teeth slamming together from the jolts.

"I remember the haze that covered the mountain. I think that means we're close," Ever said.

"We're close," Oak's voice echoed through the carriage as if he were actually inside it rather than directing it from the front. "But we're not going to make it through this magic without something."

Azure bolted upright. "What do you need?" *And it better not be a rogue emotion, bottled and ready to be reused,* she thought.

"What did you use to find Mage Lenore the first time?"

Oak asked. "It appears you're going to need that this time too. The dragons can't cross the magical barrier."

"The staff," Azure said, trying to stand up but falling onto Ever, who gingerly caught her.

"Staff. I'm on it," Manx called, trotting to Azure's bedroom in dog form.

"Don't eat it," Azure yelled, trying to peel herself off Ever. The constant bumps and sharp turns made it difficult to do, though. Ever, realizing that Azure needed help, put his hands on her hips and supported her until she got her feet under her.

Ever gave her a cautious look. "Are you good?"

Azure smiled gratefully at him. He smelled of springtime, but she didn't know why. It was like the sweetness of flowers and the freshness of new growth were mingled into one. "Yes, thank you."

Manx bounded toward her with the staff between his teeth. He stumbled a few times, but made it to her with the staff. Azure grabbed it from him, set it upright, and pushed it firmly down on the floor of the carriage. All at once the turbulence vanished and the purple-pinkish clouds disappeared, and the carriage smoothly descended.

Azure had to look out the carriage window to realize they had landed. It had been a super-smooth arrival, considering the bumpy ride. She steadied herself on the staff. She hadn't thought of pulling it out to find Mage Lenore, and apparently neither had Oak. Now she wondered how Gran would find the house, even accompanied by Gillian who had already been there once.

Through the window of the carriage Azure could tell that the grounds of Mage Lenore's house looked much as they had as before. There still the same overgrown garden bursting with fruits and vegetables, the same lopsided three-story house, and the Howling Willow, pristine and graceful.

"What in the fuckity-fuck is that?" Monet asked, pointing at something through the large windows on the other side of the carriage. Azure squinted, not sure what she was seeing clearly.

"Are those—"

"Pegasi," Ever finished.

He was right. And beside the creatures stood three figures, and then there was...

Azure sprang for the door and stumbled out of the carriage, and Oak caught her. He had just been about to open the door and help her down. There was an irritated look on his face, creating creases under his silvery eyes. "Pegasi. I wasn't told those animals would be here."

"I didn't know," Azure said, pushing off him. She'd like to stop falling on everyone.

"They annoy the dragons," Oak said.

"Oh, I'm sorry," Azure said. "Is it because they have a rivalry with other winged creatures?"

"No." Oak scoffed this like it was a ridiculous notion. "It's because Pegasi are flamboyant showoffs who shouldn't be able to fly because their egos are so damn huge."

Azure laughed. Dragons didn't like the winged horses

because they were jealous of the pristine creatures. "Well, I think dragons are far more beautiful and majestic."

Oak bowed low to Azure. "Thank you, mademoiselle. Even so, I'll keep the dragons as far from the pesky show ponies as possible."

Azure nodded before picking up her robes and running around the back of the carriage. From there she could see the three shimmering pink Pegasi, their wings folded against their bodies and their heads down, grazing. Azure's heart leapt at the sight of a small old witch handing a bridle off to a tall wizard. She bounded forward, but slowed when she realized she was about to career into Gran.

"Gran! You made it!" Azure said, excited. "I was afraid Gillian wouldn't be able to find the house."

Gran turned around, appraising Azure. She didn't open her arms to her granddaughter, but did pinch her mouth together. The young queen wanted to believe that a sentimental emotion had just passed through the old witch's heart, briefly showing on her face. "Azure, shall we discuss your clothes first or your lack of faith in my ability to find Mage Lenore?"

Azure's mouth fell open. "I just figured that Gillian—"

"I didn't need Gillian to find Mage Lenore's home," Gran said. "Now, what are you wearing?"

"They're called 'jeans.' They're super-comfortable," Azure said, pushing back her robe to show them off. "And this is a t-shirt. It's lovely."

Gran shook her head. "Comfort is what you give to your people by leading, and they want a ruler who dresses like a leader." Gran was wearing an elegant lavender silk robe adorned with rubies. A large tassel hung from the collar, where it was tied snuggly.

"It's good to see you too, Gran," Azure said, curtsying to the queen mother. It didn't matter that she was queen. If it hadn't been for this woman and her daughter, Azure wouldn't be the person she was and able to lead as she did.

From the corner of her vision Azure noticed Gillian, who had just come around one of the flying horses. "It's good to see you, Gillian."

The gnome sank into a low bow. "The pleasure is all mine, Your Majesty. I'm grateful that you're all right."

"You're going to break your back, little guy," Monet said, sidling up next to Azure.

"Monet Torrance, what have you spilled all down your front?" Gran asked him.

He looked down and then burped. "Centaur vodka. I was trying to save it, but alas! I took a bath in it instead. Not as sticky as ranch dressing, I suspect."

Gran turned her attention to Reynolds, who was on the other side of her. "You see what I mean? It's like he speaks a different language."

"Sari, you're right. I didn't understand a single word of it," Reynolds said before stepping forward and taking Azure's hand. "Queen Azure, your gran has allowed me to accompany her, and while in her company, I offer my protection as well as all of my knowledge and resources."

Azure was about to express her gratitude when Monet cut in. "Just so you know, she doesn't need anything in your pants."

Reynolds laughed nervously. "Monet, I have no idea what you mean. I'm here to protect Virgo by protecting the queen mother. It's been a long time since she's ventured from the kingdom."

"Sure, sure," Monet said, and then held up two fingers and pointed at his eyes and then at Reynolds, silently saying, "I'm watching you."

"And there's the rest of your ragtag crew," Gran said, waving at Ever, Manx, Laurel, and Finswick as they approached. She turned to Gillian. "I think it's time we showed them our little surprise, don't you?"

Gillian nodded. "Yes, I agree."

"Surprise? What surprise?" Azure asked, suddenly alarmed.

"Well, it's about Blisters," Gran began. "We weren't going to bring him, but..."

A small unicorn with rainbow hair flew around the farthest Pegasus with a giant smile on his lopsided face. Blisters swerved, then slewed sideways. His hooves scrambled in the air as he dropped straight down to fall on his side.

"That was unexpected," Monet said, suppressing a laugh.

Azure sprinted forward to help Blisters up. "You have wings! When did this happen?"

Blisters stood, shaking his head and turning around to admire his white wings, circling four times before Azure stopped him. His eyes rolled around from dizziness as he said in a squeaky voice, "Can you believe it? I woke up at half past noon and felt awfully achy." Blisters was talking so fast he wasn't pausing to breathe. "I thought it was from sleeping in Monet's bed, which is the only place I feel comfortable when you all are gone. I went to brush my teeth, and you should have seen my face when I looked in the mirror. Well, you know I dropped Monet's toothbrush right away, and I screamed. Let me reenact the moment for you. It went like this—"

Azure placed her finger to Blisters' mouth, silencing him. "This is wonderful news, Blisters. You can fly!"

"I guess we're not addressing the runt's trespassing into my personal space?" Monet asked.

"We decided to bring him along, although we would have been here significantly faster if we hadn't," Gran said, ignoring Monet.

"Clouds are cold and wet," Blisters said shaking like a dog after a bath and spraying water droplets on the crowd.

"You'll get used to flying," Azure said, petting the unicorn before standing upright. She looked at the large house, beside which the Howling Willow stood just as majestically as before. Its long branches were covered in crystals that sparkled in the waning sunlight. A soft breeze swept through and made the branches dance, creating an entrancing music.

Monet turned to Reynolds, his face tight. "Don't think about stealing anything from the Howling Willow."

Azure looked at Ever, and guilt jumped into his eyes.

"Again, I'm here simply to protect the queen mother," Reynolds said, looking offended.

Gran looked between Reynolds and Monet, her lips pursed. "One cheat telling another to behave. Now I've seen it all." She harrumphed and turned for the house. "Shall we go wake the great Mage Lenore?"

Azure sped up to walk beside Gran, who was moving

quite rapidly, even wearing her heavy traveling robe. "It's evening, not nighttime. Mage Lenore should be awake."

"When we get tired we nap, no matter what time of the day it is," Gran said.

"Oh good, you're speaking in riddles," Azure said, sarcasm dripping from her words. "Are you insinuating that there's something wrong with Mage Lenore?"

"Isn't there something wrong with everyone?" Gran asked, raising a curious eyebrow at Azure.

Monet breezed past them, heading straight for the door. "Speak for yourself, Gran." He rapped on the door three times before stepping backward.

A full minute passed before the door clicked open. Mage Lenore peered around it, her gray hair filled with curlers. She looked bewildered as she ran her sleepy eyes over Monet, and then Gran and Azure. Understanding sprang to the old witch's face.

"I almost forgot that you would be calling on me, demanding board for the night and pestering me with questions I won't answer." A smile transformed her face, instantly making it look younger.

Monet turned to Azure. "Why does the oldest witch of all time use foam curlers for her hair?" He whispered the question exceptionally loudly.

"Oh, dear," Mage Lenore said, fumbling in her apron for her wand. She pointed it at her head, and the pink curlers disappeared. Her gray hair was now in rows of perfect curls. "I was so groggy from my nap that I forgot all about my curlers. My apologies." She looked at Monet and whispered just as loudly as he had, "Spells just don't give my hair the right shape. For special company I prefer the old-fashioned approach."

Monet bowed slightly. "I'm honored that you call me 'special,' cousin."

Mage Lenore gave Monet a disgusted stare. "So, you've discussed the Torrance family with Myrtle. You and I will talk about this later. Much later." She reached out and shoved him aside. "The special company is this woman right here."

Gran held out her hand in greeting, a forced smile on her face. "Mage Lenore, I'm completely hon—"

Before she could finish her sentence, Mage Lenore pushed past her and engulfed Azure in her arms. "Dear, dear Azure, it is as the dreams foretold. You're here to learn about the Howling Willow."

Azure blanched in confusion when Mage Lenore released her. "No, Mage Lenore, I'm here because of the vampires."

The old witch nodded, dismissing her. "Blessed queen, you may *think* you know why you're here, but the reasons that brought us together are not our end objective."

Another fucking riddle. Why were old people incapable of saying things directly?

Mage Lenore moved her gaze from Azure to the person who soundlessly arrived at her side. Ever opened his mouth to say something, but Mage Lenore cut him off by holding up her hand.

"Everett, your apology isn't necessary," she began. "Did you really think I didn't know that you'd stolen a fallen branch from the Howling Willow? You could have asked for it and I'd have given it to you, since I knew how your attempts to find the Rogue Dryads would turn out."

Ever bowed his head. "I don't know what to say then, if I'm not allowed to apologize."

A warm laugh spilled from the witch's mouth, and she looked at Azure. "It appears that much like you, I make Everett speechless at times."

Azure's cheeks warmed, but she was granted a distraction when Blisters, Gillian, and Reynolds approached. Oak had remained with the dragons.

"Sari, why have you brought an uncivilized animal to sleep in my house?" Mage Lenore asked.

Gran stuttered, a strange thing for her to do. "B-B-Blisters will be on his best behavior, I assure you."

Mage Lenore turned back to her. "I wasn't referring to the unicorn. I was referring to this scoundrel." She pointed at Reynolds.

He went down on one knee in front of Mage Lenore. "It's an honor to make your acquaintance once more. I know that on our last meeting I didn't make the best impression. Please give me another chance."

Mage Lenore looked down at the wizard and her rectangular spectacles slid down her nose slightly. "That was three hundred years ago. I'm just giving you a hard time. I daresay your last-minute addition to the guest list was unexpected. We might actually have a good time now."

Reynolds stood, relief flooding his face. "Thank you, Mage Lenore. I promise never to spike your drink again."

The light expression on her face dropped. "Well, then you can't come in for the feast. I was counting on you to supply the booze for tonight's festivities."

"Tonight's festivities?" Azure asked. "We really have a lot of questions for you, and Gillian needs to review the *Book of the—*"

"Shhh there, queen. Tonight we celebrate," Mage Lenore said.

"Celebrate what?" Azure asked in bewilderment.

"The beginning of the end, of course," Mage Lenore said.

Ever gave Azure a sideways look that mirrored her confusion.

"And are you going to say that tomorrow there will be time for all our questions?" Monet asked.

Mage Lenore shook her head. "Oh, no. We will run out of time, and I'll boot you all out confused and outraged that I offered you so little insight." The old witch clapped her hands together. "You will all be simply livid with me. But tonight you have no reason to be upset, so we should eat, drink, and be merry." She turned and opened the door of her house, and a delicious aroma spilled out.

9

Azure stepped into Mage Lenore's house to find it transformed since her last visit. The comfy mismatched furniture was absent from the living room. Actually, the main area didn't look like it was inside at all. Azure stepped back outside, bumping into Ever who had been behind her, about to come into the house. He gave her a quizzical look.

"I wanted to ensure we were going into the right house," she said to him.

Ever knew exactly what Azure meant when they moved forward. His chin tilted upwards, as did everyone's as they passed over the threshold. The ceiling had disappeared, replaced by a darkening sky complete with stars twinkling overhead. Two rows of stucco buildings now stood where the furniture had once been. The colorful buildings had large balconies that looked down onto the cobbled street where they currently stood. They were decorated with flower boxes dripping with blossoms as bright as the oranges, blues, pinks, and greens of the buildings, which appeared to be homes nestled close together.

"It's like a street in Spain," Ever remarked, his voice hushed.

"New Spain, actually," Mage Lenore said, flicking her wand at the street in front of them. A row of lanterns appeared overhead, tethered between the two sets of buildings and casting colorful lights on the cobbled road under their feet.

"Mage Lenore, what is all this?" Gran asked, her usually placid face full of awe.

"I thought we'd have a little fiesta," Mage Lenore said. "I've been working on it all day. Why do you think I needed a siesta?"

"I still don't understand what we're celebrating," Azure said, striding over to the nearest building. She ran her fingers over it to ensure it was real—which it was.

Mage Lenore laughed. "She comes to her own party and doesn't even know what we're celebrating."

Laurel, who had been mostly quiet, stepped up next to Azure holding Manx in her arms in cat form. "One witch did all this?" she whispered.

Azure nodded as she took in the city street, which felt so authentic it made her head float. Finswick brushed against her leg to get her attention. "Is it possible that ML has lost her mind?" he asked, his mouth hardly parting for the words.

"Be careful, you three cats, or I won't let you sit with us," Mage Lenore said. "I'll make you sit at the kitty table."

"*Ba-dum-tss*," Monet said, pretending to play a set of drums.

"That reminds me, we are lacking something important for this celebration," Mage Lenore said.

"A knowledge of its purpose?" Azure guessed, which produced a punishing glare from Gran. She really wished that if the queen mother knew what this was about she would tell her.

"All in good time," Mage Lenore said, waving her wand at the open street. A long table and two benches materialized. Decorating its center were multiple arrangements of sunflowers and purple hydrangeas, and blue and white covered dishes filled most of the open areas. The table was bursting with color, and Azure was suddenly incredibly hungry.

"Mage Lenore, you've outdone yourself," Gran said, walking to the table and taking a whiff of one of the steaming bowls.

Mage Lenore waved her hand. "It was nothing. Just something I threw together."

The rest of the group were moving toward the table to take a seat, but Laurel was still at the queen's side. "I need a drink. Something strong," Azure said to the werecat.

Mage Lenore, who was busy telling everyone what was on the menu, looked up suddenly. "Only one drink for you, queen. You'll need your wits about you tonight."

"I'll have hers," Monet said, raising a goblet in the air.

"What you *won't* be having are the cheese enchiladas, Monet," Mage Lenore said, picking up a casserole dish and sending it in the opposite direction.

"Au contraire." Monet set down his goblet and pointed his wand at the dish to freeze it in place. "I've created a potion that fixes that whole lactose problem."

"That's nice dear, but it doesn't sound like you're aware yet of *all* of your food allergies." Mage Lenore intercepted the casserole dish and once more sent it down the table.

Disappointment sprang to Monet's face. "*More* food allergies? How is that possible?"

Mage Lenore shrugged. "Just imagine how even-tempered you'll be when you eliminate gluten, dairy, and sugar from your diet."

"Fucking miserable, that's what I'll be." Monet turned to Ever, who had taken the seat next to him. "Seriously, kill me now. There's no point in living."

Azure bent over and picked up Finswick, who was sniffing wildly. "What do you smell?"

"Fish!" he said excitedly. "She made me fish. Unlike you, she loves me."

Mage Lenore beamed in their direction as Azure and Finswick arrived at the table. "I do indeed love you, dear Finswick. It might be Azure we're celebrating tonight, but she wouldn't have this chance if not for the companionship of her trusty familiar."

Azure set Finswick down in the seat next to hers. Mage Lenore had placed a plate on the table with food for the cat. "*Arroz con pescado* for Finswick Morgan," Azure said, using his full name.

Finswick set his paws on the table in front of him and looked at Azure, eyes wide. "I don't know what you did, but you must keep doing it."

Azure tried to swallow, but that simple task was beyond her so she looked across the table at Ever. He and she were the only ones at the table who weren't busy filling the plates in front of them with food. Gran and Reynolds were already deep in a conversation about a time that he visited New Spain and ran with the minotaur.

"He had me cornered in a dead-end of a street just like this one," Reynolds said, leaning toward Sari and talking in a rush. "I pulled off my robes, which were as red as the ones that Azure is currently wearing, and waved them at the beast."

"Did that work? Did it distract the minotaur?" Gran asked.

Reynolds took a long sip of his wine and shook his head. "Hell, no! That minotaur shoved his horn so far up my—"

"Finnegan wouldn't do *what*?" Monet asked Gillian, his face red.

The gnome shrugged. "When he found out that we were leaving Virgo on this trip, he refused to restock the shop. I have no idea why."

"Well, hopefully you weren't stupid enough to tell him Reynolds was accompanying you," Monet said, running his fork through his rice but looking thoroughly uninterested in the food. He eyed the churros sprinkled with sugar with desperate longing.

Azure accepted a dish of paella, enjoying the different aromas wafting to her nose as she spooned some onto her plate.

"I can give you something to help you sleep, but you really need to find the root cause," Mage Lenore's voice traveled down the table.

Azure looked away from her food to find the old witch, who was counseling Laurel. The werecat nodded, picking at the whole fish dripping in red sauce lying on her plate.

"Are you not hungry?" Ever asked, gaining Azure's attention.

She looked up at him to find his plate still empty. "You're the one with nothing in front of you."

"I'm…worried," he admitted. Most were too engrossed in their conversation to pay them any attention. Manx and Finswick were too busy with their fish to take notice of anything going on around them on this lantern-lit New Spanish street. Strangely there was a warm breeze laced with salt, as if the coast were just on the other side of one of the rows of buildings.

"Worried?" Azure asked.

"What does Mage Lenore have planned for you?" Ever asked, leaning forward.

"I can only wonder," Azure said. She looked at her family and friends, who were happily celebrating something that was a mystery to her.

"And *I* can only wonder how it will change everything," Ever said, his blue eyes haunted.

The yawns at the table became contagious, spreading from person to person until almost everyone looked drunk from the food. Well, or in the case of Monet and Gillian, just plain drunk.

Mage Lenore clapped her hands together. "Yes, I thought that putting the sleeping potion in the food might get you off to bed at a reasonable time."

"You slipped us a sleeping potion?" Azure asked, staring down at her mostly uneaten food.

"I thought I tasted a bit of chamomile root in my dish. Nicely done," Monet said, swaying in his seat.

Mage Lenore smiled sweetly. "And no, Queen Azure, your food wasn't modified. I require your help tonight, and we need the rest of this lot to be fast asleep so they don't bother us."

The yawns continued, creating a chorus down the table. "Well, off to your rooms. Take your pick." Mage Lenore swept her hand at the villas lining the road.

"These building are real?" Gran asked.

Mage Lenore chuckled as if it were a ridiculous question. "Of course they are. You didn't think they were only for decoration?"

Monet scoffed. "Yeah, Gran, what a crazy notion! Obviously these are real villas, cause that's not completely insane since we're inside a three-story house."

Laurel was the first one to push up from the table. Like a zombie she marched off to the first villa, which was painted a rich shade of burgundy and had small palm trees in bright-blue pots flanking the door. "'Night, everyone. Think I might sleep for a year."

"No, no, no," Mage Lenore said. "You don't want to miss the trip to Lancothy tomorrow."

"Don't I?" Laurel asked as she trudged off.

"I think I'll take the purple one down the road," Gran told them. "It matches my hair."

"I knew you'd say that," Mage Lenore said. "That was why I included a huge tub enchanted with an extra-large bubble feature."

"Mage Lenore, you know me so well. I love my bubble baths," Gran said, pressing her hands to her chest.

SARAH NOFFKE

"That I do. Just don't take a bath tonight, or I fear you'll drown. Sleeping potions and baths don't mix," Mage Lenore said.

Gran nodded, then leaned over and pressed a kiss to Azure's forehead. The gesture took the girl by surprise.

"I've always been proud of you, but now more than ever I'm grateful to call you mine," she said, her lavender eyes sparkling with emotion.

"Gran, do you know what this is all about?" Azure asked, looking up at her.

"I always knew it was a possibility," Gran said.

Azure was more confused than before, but she didn't have a chance to ask another question because Gran straightened and trotted off toward her villa.

Monet was using a levitation spell to make Blisters float. He was currently snoring loudly, his tongue hanging from his mouth and his new wings limp on his back. "Where should I put this one?" he asked Mage Lenore.

"Wherever you want, but you know he'll end up with you. The villa you choose will have a bunkbed for you two," Mage Lenore said.

"But I haven't chosen one yet," Monet said, looking perplexed.

Mage Lenore didn't answer, only arched an eyebrow at him.

"You're a very strange witch," Monet said.

Finswick's food must have not been doctored either, because he was sitting on the table watching all this with wide eyes.

Manx in rabbit form hopped across the table into Ever's arms. "Take me to the black villa. It matches my soul."

Ever looked down at the pooka and shrugged before glancing at Azure. "Beats sleeping with a snoring unicorn, I guess."

She offered him a sympathetic smile. "Good night, Ever."

Reynolds and Gillian made their choices, one green and the other magenta. That left only one—the largest of them, all at the end of the street. It was blue, and perfectly matched Azure's hair.

"What about Oak?" Azure asked, picking up Finswick and rising from the table.

"He prefers to sleep with his dragons…you know that," Mage Lenore said.

"I didn't, actually. How do you always know things?" Azure was aware that it was a silly question. This was Mage Lenore, the oldest and most powerful witch on Oriceran. Still, she thought she'd chance asking.

"You know this stuff too, or you would if you allowed yourself to access it. That is one reason I chose you," Mage Lenore said, summoning a robe that had fur lining the collar. She pulled the hood over her head, looking out at Azure with a cunning stare.

Myrtle's last words before she'd kicked Azure from the shop echoed in her head: "Tell my dear cousin she's chosen well."

"Is this when you tell me what I've been chosen for?" Azure asked.

Mage Lenore pivoted and strode for the door. "This is when I show you."

10

The two moons were high in the sky when Azure and Mage Lenore exited the house. It felt bizarre to step out of the New Spanish street into the mountain air of Mage Lenore's yard. The old witch moved surprisingly fast, crossing the grounds and heading in the direction of the Howling Willow, and Azure's heart sank when the dawning started to fall on her. If she'd been honest with herself she'd have known something like this would happen, but she had been in denial. Azure set Finswick on the ground and he strolled beside her as they followed the old witch.

"Mage Lenore, is it the night of the harvest?" Azure asked, her breath misting in the cold mountain air. She pulled her robe tighter around her.

"It is, my dear queen." A bucket had materialized in Mage Lenore's hands, and it swung back and forth as she continued toward the tree.

"You don't mean for me to... I mean, you're the

protector of the Howling Willow." Azure realized she sounded cowardly. With each step closer to the giant tree, she felt more and more breathless. In the light of the moons, the crystals on the long branches sparkled like icicles. They clanged together to produce an enchanting tune, one that made Azure suddenly long for the things of her childhood. She remembered running through the long grass in the foothills with Monet. Skipping rocks by the poisoned bog, her new dress slipping into the water and catching fire. She was in her mother's arms, having just awoken from a bad dream.

That dream! She'd had it all her life. The first time it had scared her, but since then she'd longed for the replay while she slept. The blackness of her dream always gave way to a white light, and she shielded her eyes from the brightness with her arm. A tree towered over her, its branches whipping through the air. One slashed across her arm, making her stumble back. From behind her, she pulled a sword. Where had that come from? She sliced it through the air, again and again, battling the branches. When she was done she looked down at her feet, feeling immense pleasure, but she never got to see what had produced the feeling. She always awoke from the dream right then.

Mage Lenore turned and studied Azure's face. "You remember now, don't you?"

Azure felt as if she were stuck to the ground, and her mouth hung open. "The dream...was it about the Howling Willow?"

Mage Lenore gave her a smile so warm it made Azure forget the icy wind tearing through her hair. "All my life I had that same dream, up until I took my role as the protector of the last remaining Howling Willow on Oriceran." Mage Lenore held up her hand majestically, as if presenting the tree. It appeared quite elegant in the moonlight, not menacing as it had in the dream.

"You see," Mage Lenore continued, "I didn't choose you in the beginning. The tree did. It gifts that dream to witches and wizards all over Oriceran, and I, of course, got to make the final decision. It wasn't hard."

"Me?" Azure had to yell to be heard over the loud chiming of the tree. It had increased in intensity. "You've chosen me? I don't understand! You're the protector."

"And I have been for a thousand years. I was the first one chosen, because all the Howling Willows had been destroyed by those consumed with greed. However, I always knew that I wouldn't be the last. A witch, no matter how powerful, cannot live forever."

A knot suddenly rose in Azure's throat. She hardly knew Mage Lenore, and yet the idea of the witch not being alive caused her great pain. She pressed her eyelids closed and memories flashed into her mind. A young woman sailing on a ship, overlooking the waters of the Haunted sea. The same woman sharing a meal with an elegantly-dressed wizard. The woman standing in front of the Howling Willow holding a sword. No, not just any sword… the one from the dream. Azure's eyes sprang open and as a gasp shot out of her mouth.

"That was you," Azure whispered. "I saw you."

Mage Lenore smiled. "You've always had those visions of me, but now you're allowing yourself to see them."

"But how? How can I see things that haven't happened to me?" Azure asked.

"Because we're all one. And you, as the protector of the Howling Willow, are rooted to Oriceran and forever connected to all who walk it," Mage Lenore said.

"So I can know anything about anyone?" Azure asked.

Mage Lenore shook her head. "No, no. You can only know that which the Howling Willow wants you to know. It usually feels random, like a witch's shoe size or a wizard's distaste for avocados. Still, that is one of the many gifts the Howling Willow offers the chosen one."

"The other gifts? Is it the way you age? Cycling through your ages every day and living a long time because of it?" Azure asked, looking down at Finswick. He had the strangest expression, like he'd just eaten an exploding canary by accident.

"I was called to the Howling Willow when I was hundreds of years older than you are now," Mage Lenore told her, speaking loudly. The crystals' chiming was now more like loud angry clanging. "The way I age is the gift the tree gave me, and I'm being completely honest when I say that I don't know what the tree has in store for you, Queen Azure. You see, I've found that the relationship that the Howling Willow has with its protector is a personal one. It will be like your familiar— close to you and connected in every way, and also a bit of a pain in the ass." She looked at the Howling Willow. "I'm getting to that. Quiet down for a moment, would you?" The tree didn't quiet down. Rather, it swung its branches with more ferocity, making them blur in the wind.

"This is all so unexpected. I never would have

thought…" Azure's voice trailed away as her mind was overwhelmed with all the reasons this wouldn't work.

"You're not happy to have been chosen," Mage Lenore observed. "That was me once. I thought my role as the protector would isolate me, but I've found the opposite to be true. After harvest, I deliver wands to many throughout Oriceran. The magic of the tree makes this possible. My connection to the Howling Willow allows me to know the young witches and wizards. Since taking on my role, I've never felt lonely."

"But I have a kingdom to rule," Azure argued. "Virgo needs me."

Mage Lenore nodded. "So does the Howling Willow. There is more magic in this one tree than the entire universe, and it has entrusted that power and its guardianship to you. I understand your reservations, but there is no greater honor than what you've been chosen for."

"But why was I chosen?" Azure asked.

"The tree blessed you with the dream because you had the right aptitude for the job. You're pure of heart, and won't abuse the power it wields." Mage Lenore paused, a knowing smile springing to her mouth. "*I* chose you because when I look at you I see myself."

"Well, thank you, but—"

"You're assuming this is a compliment," Mage Lenore cut Azure off. "I'm stubborn…so much so that I traveled to the Haunted Sea even though my parents forbade it. I'm overly careful with my heart, and withheld it from the man you saw me dining with, afraid of falling in love and losing. I see these characteristics in you, Azure."

"Oh, well, I guess—"

Mage Lenore interrupted a second time. "And much like you, I am brave, fierce, and will sacrifice everything for the greater good of my people. Queen Azure, I chose you because I knew you were the right one to protect the Howling Willow. Yes, it will demand much from you, but you have that much to give."

Azure stared down at Finswick. His eyes were wide, and without a doubt he knew what Azure was thinking right then. She drew in a breath and dropped to one knee, bowing her head. "I'm honored to have been chosen, by both you and the Howling Willow. I take my role to protect magic seriously, and from this day forward my life belongs to the tree."

"Oh, Merlin's beard! Hell, no." Mage Lenore laughed. "You're not kicking me out just yet. I've still got time on this planet."

Azure flipped her head up, gasping. "I'm sorry. I just thought—"

Mage Lenore was still laughing as she cut Azure off. "Your willingness to drop everything and take on this role is exactly why you're the right person. Your time to protect the tree will come soon, but I daresay you have a mission that demands your attention right now. I'm not sure what the parameters of your guardianship will look like. Maybe you'll live here in the house built from Howling Willow." Mage Lenore waved a hand at the three-story house that was the strangest and most wonderful place Azure had ever seen. "And maybe you'll rotate through your ages each day as I do. I cannot say. But when the time comes—when I die, which will be fairly soon—you will take on my role as the protector of magic."

Azure swallowed, unsure if she should be happy or sad or completely confused.

"But before any of that, you should meet the tree that has visited your dreams every night since you were born," Mage Lenore said, holding her arm out to the Howling Willow.

"Is this when you teach me how to harvest?" Azure asked.

Mage Lenore smiled at her as if she were a special-needs chimpanzee. "Oh, queen, we both know that you've been learning how to do that all your life. The harvest is not something another person can teach a true protector. The tree has been showing you what men didn't know for centuries. They cut down the Howling Willows willy-nilly and then wondered why the wood died after some time, taking with it the magic. But you know how to harvest it the right way, so that its magic never dies. You know how to do it so that the tree will never be overconsumed."

Azure took a step toward Mage Lenore and Finswick followed, but the old witch held up a hand.

"You may stay, Azure, but you, Finswick Morgan, must remain here," Mage Lenore said. "What the young queen must do now, she does on her own."

Finswick hadn't said a word since this strange adventure started. He looked up at Azure and sort of smiled in that way he did when he was serenely happy. "Neither the tree nor Mage Lenore could have chosen a better witch."

Azure was unable to say anything, so she simply nodded her appreciation to her cat. She raised her chin high and strode toward the tree, which was still waving in the wind and making gentle music.

As she neared the ancient tree she felt a draw, as if it were pulling her in with a cord. Memories washed over her. Mostly they were her own, but many belonged to others. Flashes streaked across her vision, many going back to the prehistoric age. This tree had been here since the beginning. The Howling Willow was as old as time.

Azure knelt when she was close to the tree, but maintained a safe distance. "I'm honored to serve you, Majestic Howling Willow."

The chimes from the crystals on its branches had been playing a song, but suddenly it had lyrics.

Azure Lydia Vladar...so we officially meet. I will always honor you, protect you, and provide that which you need. You know what is expected of you in return, correct? the tree chimed in her head.

"I'm to protect you from others and harvest your branches for wands once a month. Is there anything else?" Azure stood up, staring at the willow's branches as they swayed.

You've forgotten the most important part of your job, the tree sent.

Azure's face scrunched in confusion. "What's that?"

As with all loved ones, you must tolerate me at my worst and battle me to bring out the very best. Mothers do it with children, and children do the reverse with their parents. We all have demons inside us, but thankfully we also have those who love us unconditionally. The morning after, you will have to forgive me for what I become on the full moon.

Suddenly the moons seemed to swing high into the sky, casting a bright glow on the Howling Willow. It lifted its branches into the air and then froze. Azure tensed, remembering the dream. She clambered backward, but not in time. The branches swung down at her as one and a howl screeched through the air. One of the branches caught her across the arm, searing it with mind-numbing pain. She clapped a hand over the wound and turned to Mage Lenore, her insides jittering.

"I don't... I don't have the sword! What do I do?" Azure screamed. In the dream she'd always had it—the sword that appeared from seemingly nowhere—but presently all she had was her wand.

"The Howling Willow gave you your sword long ago," Mage Lenore called, her words more in Azure's mind than verbalized.

Azure ducked the tree's multiple assaults. It was howling so loudly now that she was sure her ears would explode. *The Howling Willow already gave me the sword*? she wondered frantically.

Azure dove to the ground as branches swung over her. *The tree was going to kill her!* Fuck protecting it! She was the one who needed protection from this damn monster.

Azure rolled onto her stomach and pushed to a crouch. The tree's branches were sticking eerily straight up in the air—which just meant it was planning its next assault, she knew instinctively.

The Howling Willow hadn't given her a sword. The staff she had received was made from its wood, but that was in the carriage. And then, of course, there was her wand...

Azure felt as if the breath had been sucked out of her, and she tensed as the Howling Willow's branches swung all at once. It reminded her of a toddler throwing a tantrum.

Carefully, without any sudden movements, she reached for the wand in her robes. She nearly had her hand around it when the branches shot into the air again and whipped violently, and Azure ducked as she withdrew her wand— which was strangely heavy, requiring both hands. Her eyes widened in shock as she stared at the giant sword she had removed from her robe, then she stood and raised the silver and blue sword above her head.

The tree's branches spiraled toward her. Azure caught them with the sword, cutting off the ends, which clattered to the ground. Again and again she parried the tree's blows with the sword, countering each of the assaults. For what felt like a lifetime the two sparred, which eventually became more of a dance rather than a fight.

The howling was all at once replaced by the most peaceful silence Azure had ever enjoyed as the Howling Willow grew still, its branches not even swaying in the gentle breeze. Just like that, it was over. Azure stared downward as she had in the dream. Branches covered in crystals lay in a neat arrangement at her feet.

Azure sucked in a breath. The crystals suddenly receded into the wood, sealing their magic deep into the branches where it would be sealed there forever. Azure had successfully harvested the Howling Willow, and knew this would not be her last time.

11

Monet and Ever stared across the table at their queen. She'd awakened that morning in the blue villa to their incessant knocking. When she'd stood up from the four-poster bed, she'd found that every muscle in her body ached.

Azure had refused to say a word to them until she had eaten something, since she thought the lack of food was starting to catch up with her. Strangely, as soon as she'd felt the craving for food, the dining room table in the living area of the villa had been stocked with fruit, juice, tea, fresh steaming-hot bread, and other good things.

Damn, the Howling Willow is badass! she thought, grabbing a piece of bread and spreading strawberry jam on it.

"What do you mean *you're* the new protector of the Howling Willow?" Monet asked in astonishment after she'd hastily confessed.

Azure crammed the toast into her mouth and said

between chews, "Just that. I was chosen, so when Mage Lenore passes I will take her place."

"But we can still party, right?" Monet asked.

Azure nearly choked on the orange juice she was drinking to wash down the bread. "Of course that's your concern! A tree tried to kill me." She pointed to her bandaged arm. That was about as much as she could say, and she knew it at her core. Only the protector could know the details of the harvest—that was one way the Howling Willow was protected.

"Let me take a look at that." Monet had the bandage off before Azure could protest.

She noticed that Ever looked as if he were mourning a loss. His head hung, and his lips were pinched together at an odd angle.

"I don't know how my new role will change my life. I presume I'll still be queen, but I honestly don't know. If necessary I'll give my mother back the crown, because nothing is more important than protecting the Howling Willow," Azure stated, trying to make Ever feel better.

He brought his eyes up to meet hers. "It's a huge responsibility, and the greatest honor I could ever imagine. Your path has been chosen." A pained smile etched itself onto his lips. "Selfishly, I worry how this changes your future."

Monet whipped his head up to stare at Ever before looking at Azure. "Oh man, you're right. You're pretty much married to that tree for the rest of your life."

The toast churned uncomfortably in Azure's stomach, so she sat up and cleared her throat. "Well, for now I'm still queen of Virgo, and I'm on a mission to stop vampires. I will not think of my future role as protector until that time comes."

Ever nodded, trying to inject strength into the movement. "It really is the most amazing thing to ever happen to someone. I can only imagine the power you wield now."

Azure nodded, leaning forward excitedly. "You have no idea. I'm connected to the tree, which is deeply rooted into Oriceran, which connects me to *everything*. I now understand how Mage Lenore knows so much." Azure waved her hands at the villa around them. "This house, her life, the strangeness of this mountain... I know how it all works, and that power flows in me." A sharp pain shot through her arm. "Ouch!" She shot a look at Monet, who was messing with her wound.

"That power is also enough to kill you," Monet said, standing back with a serious look on his face.

"What?" Azure said, looking down at the wound she'd bandaged last night. Green slime dripped from the laceration, and she instantly felt light-headed.

"Is she okay?" Ever asked, darting around the table.

"Well, I'm pretty sure the tree's assaults could be her end, but not this time." Monet looked at Azure and laid a gentle hand on her shoulder. "I'll be right back. I have a potion that will combat the poison, but you're going to owe me big for saving your life...again."

Azure drew in a breath. "Put it on my tab."

Monet left without another word. Ever stared at Azure's wound and then at her face.

"This will one day make you Mage Azure, you realize."

"Oh my." Azure clapped a hand to her mouth and

swayed, thinking she'd pass out. The poison must be getting to her.

"I'm really happy for you," Ever said, but there was something in his voice that was distinctly *un*happy.

And then in a flash, Azure saw it. Saw the man before her as a child, as a young boy, as a man, and knew without a doubt what she had long suspected. Ever had been inexplicably and relentlessly in love with her from the very beginning.

Azure opened her eyes and stared at the man before her, the one who made her feel safe. Who made her feel alive. If she allowed herself to feel such things, there would be a confession right then. However, Azure realized that, much like Mage Lenore, she must be careful with her heart.

"I've been able to decipher enough of the *Book of the Dead* to know that we need more. There's simply not enough here to go on. I need the other pages," Gillian told Azure, looking up from the large table where they'd enjoyed last night's meal.

"Manx, would you mind not pecking at that bagel right next to the ancient page?" Azure asked, shooing the raven form of the pooka away. Her arm had felt better instantly after drinking the potion Monet gave her. He'd burst back through the villa door, saving her from thinking about her heart or Ever's.

Manx raised his head from the onion bagel and stared at Azure blankly. "Queen, if you knew anything about anything, you'd know that the page can't be destroyed." He thrust his beak straight down into the page, puncturing it.

"Manx!" Azure scolded, picking up the bird, who morphed into a giant black dog, whom she dropped. She fell backward and landed hard on her injured arm as Manx bounded off barking.

"He never gets tired of that joke," Ever said, helping Azure up.

"The page, though. Is it..." Azure stood to find Gillian holding the page in the air. It was free from any punctures.

The gnome smoothed his stubby hand over the page after laying it back down. "The pooka is indeed correct, which is why the original founder vampires stole the pages and scattered them. They couldn't destroy the book, but they could keep the relevant information from those who wanted to end vampirism."

Gran, who looked more refreshed than she had in the last ten years, strode over smiling broadly. She spread her arms wide. "Oh, my dear Azure. When all this is yours, I'm moving in with you."

"Azure's?" Gillian asked. Reynolds and Laurel had just joined them, and were grabbing various breakfast foods from bowls.

Gran wrapped an arm around Azure's shoulder and squeezed her. It wasn't just a rare thing for Gran to do but awkward, since she was a head taller than the old woman. "The queen of Virgo will be the next protector of the Howling Willow. Won't you, my dear?"

Gillian startled to a standing position, lost his balance on the bench where he stood and toppled over. Reynolds dropped his blueberry muffin onto his plate, of which it bounced and rolled to the ground to join Gillian. Manx, in dog form, darted after it, and Laurel let out a sudden shriek that sounded like a muffled meow.

From the ground, Gillian emerged, his hands and head peeking up around the bench. "Please, Queen Mother, don't make such jokes."

Gran laughed. "I'd never joke about such a thing. I knew it since the first time you had that dream, my child. I told your mother then that it was a sign you were on the list."

"You knew," Azure said in disbelief.

"She knows everything, apparently," Reynolds said, picking up another muffin.

"This makes you the most powerful witch on all of Oriceran," Laurel said, her paws on her face.

"Not yet it doesn't," Azure stated. "Right now we have a vampire problem which could ruin all magic if we don't stop it."

"That was why Mage Lenore had Myrtle give you the necklace," Ever said in a hushed voice.

Azure turned to him. "You're right—that makes more sense now."

"Speaking of the crazy old loon, where is she?" Monet asked, looking around.

"She's delivering wands," Azure stated. "She said I could harvest before taking the position formally, but not deliver the wands since I'm not fused enough with the power to know which one goes to which person."

Gran pointed at the table, conjuring a magnum of champagne. "Glory be to Merlin! This is the best day of my life." The old witch bounced over and filled a champagne flute—which she also conjured—to the brim before drinking it merrily.

Azure wanted to laugh, but the weight of her new role and how it would affect her life weighed too much on her. Instead she turned to Gillian, who was regarding her like she was the Howling Willow itself. "You said you needed more pages, is that right?"

He seemed to wake from his daze and brought his eyes to the page from the *Book of the Dead*. "Yes, that's right. This cuts off at a crucial part, so it really doesn't give me much to work with."

Gran and Monet were already on their second glass of champagne and were giggling like clowns. "We can make her enchant the house to be a rollercoaster! We'll ride it continuously, and I'll bet you puke first," Gran said.

"Game on, old woman," Monet replied, taking another sip before belching loudly.

"Focus, people. Vampires. *Book of the Dead*. We need more pages," Azure snapped at the pair.

Gran swiveled her gaze to Azure and smiled. "No problem. I'll go to New Egypt and find them."

"Sari!" Reynolds said, shocked.

"What?" Gran hiccupped. "We need more pages. Someone needs to find them. Azure has her hands full going to Lancothy to get bats...oh, and being the new protector of the Howling Willow!" She caroled the last part gleefully.

"But there are *vampires* in New Egypt. I can't risk you getting bitten," Reynolds argued.

"Too bad," Gran said, draining her glass. "What's life without a bit of danger?"

"This is too dangerous!" Reynolds insisted.

Gran set down her glass and stuck her fists on her hips. "If Azure is willing to give up her life to protect the biggest source of magic on Oriceran, I think I can muster enough courage to enter New Egypt and hunt for some dusty old pages." Gran turned around, seeking Gillian. "Will you accompany me—if you're not too scared?"

Gillian straightened, his face falling into a neutral expression. "Absolutely. That's the job that needs to be done, and I think I know exactly where to look first, based on where this one was found."

Gran nodded curtly before turning around. "There you go. We're going to New Egypt. Now, Reynolds, you came on this expedition to protect me. Are you going to stay on your mission, or are you a coward who only came to pursue me without any risks?"

The color drained from Reynolds' face, and he looked around the group. Everyone's eyes were on him. "I-I-I-I'm here to protect you, no matter the risks. Pursuit is a secondary goal…if I prove myself worthy of such a thing."

12

After Gran and the others left Azure had fewer distractions. She found it difficult to not look directly at Ever. From his tentative glances she guessed that he sensed she felt awkward. She was certain he didn't know what she'd discovered about his feelings. Azure also assumed he'd been trying to find the right way to confess them, but when had there been time between saving Virgo and stopping vampires?

The door to Mage Lenore's house slammed shut and the witch herself leaned against it, exhaustion making her face long.

"Mage Lenore, are you all right?" Azure hurried over and grabbed the old woman's arm, sensing she was having a hard time holding herself up.

She looked up at Azure, her eyes brimming with stress. "That was my last harvest. This old body just can't do it again. Just the deliveries nearly took me out!"

Ever arrived on the other side of Mage Lenore and helped Azure lead her over to the table, but before they could lower her into a seat she turned abruptly to Azure, waving them off.

"I'm fine. I'm fine, but we're running out of time," Mage Lenore said, her voice growing squeaky like that of a young child. "I get an extension on the nights I deliver wands, but soon I'll change to my youngest form and then I won't have access to my magic."

"Access to your magic? Why do you need that?" Azure asked.

"You need to get to Lancothy, don't you? And you're running out of time." Mage Lenore pulled her wand from her traveling robe and began swirling it.

"Wait, you haven't answered any of my questions yet!" Azure said, holding up her hands.

Mage Lenore paused, a slight smile lighting her ancient face. Centuries of wisdom made the depths of her eyes feel endless. "I warned you how this was going to go."

Monet, who had polished off a plate of bacon, wiped his mouth and rose from the table. "I was paying attention. You're not answering any of our questions, and leaving us frustrated and completely unsatisfied."

Mage Lenore turned to Monet. "Son of Zander Torrance, you're just as astute as your father."

Monet trotted over and draped his arm around Mage Lenore's shoulder. "And you know that because he's your cousin?"

Mage Lenore patted Monet on the cheek. "Wouldn't you like to know."

"But you are full of information and short on time. I

know your game," Monet said, looking at Azure. "Ready to blow this taco stand?"

Azure shook her head. "Mage Lenore, the vampires… Do you know how we can eradicate them?"

Mage Lenore's gaze fell on the ruby hanging from Azure's neck. "I gave you a necklace that protects you from the virus. That's all I can offer you. Your search for a cure is a part of your journey. Giving you that information would deprive you of the opportunity to find it on your own."

Manx, who had eaten the centerpieces on the breakfast table while in goat form, hopped off and trotted over. "You're a frustrating old witch."

Mage Lenore peered affectionately down at the pooka. "Why, thank you very much!"

Laurel, with Finswick in her arms and Blisters trailing behind her, joined the group. "So we're leaving now?"

"That you are," Mage Lenore answered, swirling her wand and giving Azure one last look. "I'll be seeing you very soon, Queen Azure, for the very last time."

Azure choked on her tears as she fell into a spiral of wind and colors and the New Spanish street vanished.

The group found themselves on a green hill in the same positions they had been in at Mage Lenore's house.

The carriage, Oak, and the dragons were beside them. The dragons tossed their heads, disoriented. "What happened? Where are we?" Oak asked.

Monet laughed. "Lancothy. Mage Lenore decided to

send us using a relocating spell. Don't eat any heavy carbs for eight hours, and it's normal if your feet swell slightly."

Azure turned to Monet. "I thought only members of the Torrance family could relocate."

"It appears that Mage Lenore can make others relocate as well. And honestly, I don't know if it's just those from the Torrance family or what since that sneaky witch won't tell me," Monet said, turning in a circle to take in the land of Lancothy. It was his first time in the kingdom, and the awe on his face accurately expressed how incredible the scenery truly was.

"Far out," Blisters said, leaning into Monet like he was having trouble standing upright.

Lancothy was located inside a mountain that the were-animals who populated it had carved it out. Sunlight slipped through gaps in the mountain and from the giant hole at the top. Rolling hills spread across the vast land, which was dotted with cottages, farms, a city center, and a castle.

Azure spun around, getting her bearings. They were on the outskirts, just beside the exit through the mountain. A ladder led to the cave that took visitors in and out of the kingdom. That was where the bats would be found, according to Azure's last visit. She was grateful Mage Lenore had put them directly into the kingdom so they didn't have to brave the bats.

"Are we safe out here in the open?" Ever asked, on high alert.

"Yes, Gran cleared it with the Lancothy officials," Azure explained. "She set it up under the pretense of the royal tour I was on before this vamp mess started."

"Lorde still won't like it," Laurel warned, referring to the thug who had tried to kill Azure and Ever the last time they were here. "You need to be extra-careful. That werebear doesn't play by the rules, and he might have been successful at overthrowing the government since I left."

Laurel's eyes skirted nervously over the city in the distance, and her claws slid in and out several times.

"Are you all right?" Azure asked.

"Yes," Laurel said at once. "I mean no. Actually, I'm fine —it's just that being back here in my homeland is strange."

"Not to mention that you left without permission, and pretty much look like a deserter to a population of wereanimals who don't like the outside world," Monet said coolly.

"You're rather tactless," Azure said, reproving her best friend with a single look.

"Undeniably, I am," Monet admitted. "And we could stand around not getting anything done or we could be straight with each other, which will make everything easier."

"Okay, fine," Azure said. "Laurel, you don't have to go to the city center with us. Actually, it would be best if you, Manx, and Blisters went after the bats. Would you, please? It's really too dangerous for Monet or Ever to be around them."

Laurel nodded, looking relieved not to have to go to the city where judging eyes would dwell on her. "Yes, we'll get them for you."

"Good, and be sure to get inside before nightfall. Gran rented one of those cottages over there for us to stay in." Azure pointed to a cluster of stone buildings on a hill in the distance. She turned to the group gathered around her.

"That warning goes for everyone. We must *all* be inside before sunset."

"The dragons hunt at night," Oak said.

"Not in Lancothy they don't," Azure said. "Werewolves own the night here."

Oak scoffed at this, leaning down to run his large hand over the head of one of his dragons. "Werewolves make a fantastic meal."

"You can't harm the werewolves," Laurel explained. "The land of Lancothy was cursed long ago when my people shut us inside this mountain to get away from the world. The werewolves get the night, and if we harm them the mountain destroys itself."

"Hmmm, well, then I guess we can be flexible," Oak said, standing back from the dragons. He pointed to the sky that was visible through the hole in the top of the mountain and spoke in a strange language. Three of the dragons threw their heads up and unfolded their wings, then took off, soaring up to the top of the mountain.

"Why didn't that one go?" Monet asked.

Oak looked down at the majestic dragon. "Micky says she wants to stay with the queen."

Monet looked at Azure and from the corner of his mouth he said loudly, "I didn't hear Micky say a damn thing."

Azure didn't know what to think about the dragon wanting to remain with her. That seemed strange. She'd kept her distance from the dragons so far, not that she wasn't curious about them.

"What do you want us to do with the bats?" Laurel asked.

"Just find them and protect them the best you can," Azure ordered. "I'm going to meet with the officials about putting guards on the caves. That would be the best option."

"Mademoiselle," Oak interrupted. "I must ask that you accompany me to the castle."

"What? Why?" Azure asked.

"You want a weredragon scale. Well, I'm here to help you obtain it," Oak replied.

"But you said you could get it and I couldn't," Azure said, confused. "Shouldn't she be working on finding the way to bottle the emotion of true love for Oak instead of accompanying him on his mission for her?"

"I did say that, but although the weredragons will give me a scale, they will know it's not for me. I assume they will want to meet the person I'm giving the scale to," Oak continued, "and I suspect there will be other benefits to your accompanying me."

Monet leaned close to Azure. "Don't you just love the mystery in his voice?"

In fact Azure didn't appreciate that Oak, like Mage Lenore, was up to something but not being honest about it. Finally she nodded though, and turned to Monet and Ever. "Will you two go as diplomats and meet with the officials? We need them to set up fulltime guards on the bats."

Ever agreed at once with a nod.

"And don't," Azure began, her eyes pinned on Monet. "I repeat, *don't* insult any of the wereanimals. No name-calling."

Monet's shoulders dropped a bit. "You ruin everything."

Azure turned to the group, scanning their faces. "Okay,

we all have our missions. Stay safe, and we'll meet at the cottage before sunset."

Everyone nodded before moving off in different directions.

13

The zombie stood in the shadows of the cliff watching the group as they split up. He could smell his target. For miles he'd trekked across Oriceran, drawn to the person. The drive to get to her and bite her was all he could feel. Anyone who got in his way would be destroyed.

The zombie clawed at his skin, unable to control the nervous rage inside. It had exploded many times during the journey, and he had left dead in his wake. Soon his mission would be complete so he could once again rest.

The target was walking in the direction of a castle, flanked by a man and a dragon.

"Do you want to tell me what this is about?" Azure asked Oak.

The wizard lit his long pipe as they walked. She was very interested in the dragon casually striding beside her.

The Baltic Long-tooth dragons weren't large when their wings were folded into their bodies—about the size of a pony—but definitely bigger than Blisters, who was more the size of a large poodle.

The ragged breathing of the dragon was loud, sounding like sandpaper rubbing on a surface. Her horn-studded tail gracefully swung behind her. She looked up at Azure, blinking her yellow eyes impassively.

Oak didn't reply to Azure's question, and she kept talking. "I really should be the one to meet with the Lancothy officials. They are expecting me, so I'm not sure how they will respond to Monet and Ever. We're not wholeheartedly welcomed here."

Laurel had told Azure when they had first met that the wereanimals thought the people of Oriceran held great prejudice against them. That was why the elders had built their kingdom inside of the mountain of Lancothy. They stayed away from the prejudice, afraid of the outside world. Lorde, the leader of a rebel group, wanted to fight the prejudice, retaliating against the world outside the mountain for perceived abuses. It was an extremely sensitive area, and one that Azure desperately wanted to help with.

"I suspect that Ever and Monet, whose advice you trust and whose protection you value, will do fine handling the officials," Oak said, taking a long pull on the pipe.

The dragon kept looking over her shoulder at the cliff and cave in the distance.

"I do trust them, but I'm not sure why you insisted I accompany you. I'd prefer total honesty. Why did you say that Micky wanted to stay with me?" Azure asked.

Oak halted, swinging around to face the direction of the cave, his eyes narrowed. "You can't see it, but Micky smells a beast. It's stalking you, and Monet and Ever would not be successful in protecting you from it, I'm afraid."

Azure's eyes widened, unblinking. "A beast? You mean a wereanimal?"

"No, not a wereanimal." Oak shook his head, spinning back around and stalking toward the castle in the distance. Azure kept looking for this beast, but all she saw was grass and rocks.

Oak had gone a fair distance when Azure turned to find that Micky hadn't left her side. "You're really protecting me? From what?" she asked the dragon, who simply stared back at her with glowing eyes.

Azure sprinted forward and caught up with Oak. "Only those from Lancothy and those given permission can enter this land. Nothing else can get in here."

Oak laughed, which caused him to cough. He slapped his chest. "Those rules only apply to the living."

"What? The beast that is following me is dead?" Azure asked.

The castle was only a few yards away now. "Yes, zombies are dead, and therefore can't be killed. You would be wise to stay as close to Micky as possible."

Azure's throat closed and her hands shook as she lifted them to her chest, trying to breathe past the sudden fear. She stared into the distance again. "A zombie? But that's forbidden magic! How—"

"I'm fairly certain that vampires don't play by the rules, nor do the ones forced to work for them," Oak said, his voice growing fainter as he got closer to the castle.

Ata. Azure knew at once that the powerful wizard had been forced to create a zombie, which wouldn't stop until it had her.

The dragon was still pacing dutifully by her side, although Oak had disappeared into the castle. Azure said, "Thank you. Your protection has saved my friends, and now me."

"Okay, I got another one for you," Monet declared, unwrapping a strawberry-flavored Laffy Taffy. "How do you get an alien baby to sleep?"

Ever thought for a moment and then shook his head. "How?"

Monet squinted at the answer written on the candy wrapper. "You rocket. I don't get it. Why is it spelled like that?"

Ever laughed, grabbing the wrapper. "'Rocket,' like a spaceship. It's how aliens would travel to Oriceran."

"But you travel to other planets and don't take a rocket, or whatever it's called," Monet argued.

"It's just a thing on Earth. They have ships that can go into outer space," Ever explained.

Monet's eyes widened. "Wow. I want a ship!"

"Oh yeah? I think every guy does at some point," Ever said, remembering his love for science fiction when he was on Earth. It had mostly disappeared on Oriceran, since magic was real.

"If I had a ship I'd call it…" Monet thought for a moment and then said, "Ricky Bobby."

A laugh burst from Ever's mouth. "That's a strange name. Why wouldn't you call it something powerful, like ArchAngel?"

Monet shrugged. "I just like the sound of it. 'Ricky Bobby,'" he sang, pulling another Laffy Taffy from his pocket. "I got another one."

Ever looked over his shoulder, searching for Azure, but she'd disappeared. He wished she hadn't gone with Oak. Although he trusted the dragon-tamer, he worried about Azure when she wasn't nearby. Something in the air had felt different lately, something that her necklace couldn't protect her from. That was just a feeling, though, and Ever couldn't support it with fact.

Monet cleared his throat, opening the wrapper as they moved closer to the city. They would no doubt attract the attention of everyone there. That was another reason Ever wished Azure was there. She'd been granted access to the city, but they were only her cabinet members and could suffer from the brutal prejudice of the wereanimals of Lancothy.

"What is a parasite?" Monet asked, his green eyes looking at Ever with curiosity.

"I don't know," Ever said, staring vigilantly around as they approached the gates. A weretiger blocked the way into the city.

"I don't get it again. It says, 'Something you see in Paris,'" Monet said, popping the candy into his mouth.

"It's a city on Earth," Ever explained.

"Well, that's a dumb joke," Monet said. "What's the big deal with this Paris place that it gets put into a joke?"

"It's considered a romantic city. That's one of the

reasons, I suspect." Ever changed topics, indicating the weretiger. "I think we might have some trouble with this guy. I recognize him from before. He's one of Lorde's crew."

"Maybe he's just in need of a good joke," Monet said, pulling another piece of candy from his robes.

"Then we're screwed," Ever said.

"Ha-ha. I see my attempts at entertainment are lost on you. You're simply ungrateful," Monet said.

"The city of Lancothy is closed to your type," the weretiger said, his voice loud.

Ever and Monet halted only a few feet away. "We were invited by your council as members of the party of the Queen of Virgo."

"We in Lancothy don't recognize your queen," the weretiger said.

"Under the decree of the formal council—"

A bolt of white light hit the weretiger straight between the eyes and the large animal crumpled on the cobbled path.

Monet had his wand out and a satisfied look on his face. "What did you do that for?" Ever asked.

"We both know that wasn't going to end well. I just saved us time," Monet said, pocketing his wand.

Ever stared down at the unconscious weretiger. Monet was probably right. It would have resulted in a fight, so they'd now avoided all the drama. Ever held up his hands and drew power from the ground under their feet. Symbols lit up on the backs of his hands and arms and he placed a simple charm on the weretiger, cloaking him so that he wouldn't be spotted until he awoke. That would buy them some time with Lorde's group.

"Good thinking," Monet said, stepping over the now-invisible figure of the weretiger. "Now let's go shake things up."

Laurel panted as she climbed the long ladder to the cave. She was grateful that she'd been excused from entering the city. The idea of going into Lancothy after she'd fled with Queen Azure filled her sleep with nightmares. Lorde would find a way to punish her, or the officials could imprison her for breaking the supreme law that stated no wereanimal could leave the mountain. Worse than all that would have been the shame. No one was supposed to *want* to venture outside of Lancothy, where the rest of Oriceran would openly judge them. It had been drilled into her head all her life.

There were wereanimals, and everyone else. "Us against them," the preacher would state at church services. "We live inside these walls because our ancestors suffered much abuse. We will not! We endure the reign of the wolves at night, knowing that the curse is far better than the prejudice we'd encounter outside these borders."

Laurel had never agreed with this mindset, but speaking against the church and government wasn't something any sane wereanimal did. Instead, Laurel had kept her head down and her beliefs to herself. For a long time she'd drowned her desire to travel the planet, telling herself that such aspirations were futile. But now she'd explored, seeing the gorgeous valleys of Virgo and the deserts of New Egypt, and she'd been to the top of the Mountain of Truth and met the great Mage Lenore.

Listen to your dreams, because anything is possible, she told herself as she climbed higher.

"Do you need a lift?" Manx asked, hovering beside her.

She chanced taking a hand off the ladder to swat at him. "Get out of here."

"Climbing all the way to the cave must be a pain," Manx said, sounding not at all sympathetic.

"I enjoy the exercise," Laurel lied.

"Whatever you do, don't look down," Manx cautioned. "If you fall from here you'll break a limb for sure."

"When I get to the top I'm roasting a rabbit for lunch," Laurel said through gritted teeth.

Blisters peeked his head over the edge. "That flight didn't take very long," the unicorn said and flapped his wings, which made him rise into the air and nearly fall off the cliff. He scrambled to safety, sending rocks and dirt over the side and down onto Laurel. She clung to the ladder, pressing her eyes shut and holding her breath.

"Damn it, would you two mind not making my job harder?" Laurel spat. It was only about ten more feet to the top.

"I've considered your request, werecat, and the answer is no," Manx said. "It is programmed into my DNA to create mischief. It literally pains me to be good...and then there's that dysfunctional unicorn. There's no helping him, so you're pretty much screwed."

"Come on, guys," Blisters called over the edge. "It's dark up here, and I think there's something watching me. Oh, and there's a funny smell, but that might be me because I haven't bathed in a few weeks and I think I stepped in dragon poop. But seriously, hurry up! I see eyes in the dark."

"Go help him," Laurel ordered Manx.

"Why we brought an accident-prone unicorn with us into a slippery and dark cave, I have no idea," Manx said, flapping his wings to fly up to the mouth of the cave.

Manx might pretend he didn't like having Blisters around, but Laurel knew the truth. If something happened to any of them, they'd be glad they had Blisters. Every part of him could be used to heal. The unicorn couldn't perform magic, but just like Manx, he was made of magic. Laurel wished the same were true of her, but she was only a werecat. There was nothing special about her, except that she had two sets of DNA and was tightly tied to both.

14

Azure checked over her shoulder. She was largely powerless against zombies. They could be blasted with a spell, but they would keep coming—which was why creating zombies had been outlawed.

Her dragon bodyguard regarded her with a thoughtful stare as she asked, "Shall we go meet some weredragons?"

Micky just blinked up at her, a wisdom in the dragon's eyes similar to what Azure had seen in Mage Lenore's.

She turned toward the castle entrance, feeling odd entering the building alongside a dragon. Her life just kept getting stranger. Azure wasn't sure if she was more surprised by her escort or what it was protecting her from. Zombies and dragons... It seemed silly to her that months ago she had found it hard to accept that she was half-human. That was the least unusual part of her life now.

Torches lined the arched entryway. Its walls were covered in bright green moss, and the smell of smoke was heavy in the air. Ahead the entrance gave way to a large courtyard from which loud noises could be heard.

Micky froze in the shadows of the entryway and Azure turned back to her, wondering if she should stay back as well. She blinked at the dragon, unsure what to say. It wasn't like she could understand the dragon, or vice versa. And then, quite clearly, she heard a voice in her head say, *Go.*

A dragon's roar made Azure jump, and when she swiveled to face the sound she felt something nudge her back. Micky was looking at her intently.

Okay, just when Azure thought things couldn't get weirder, they did. She nodded at the dragon and pivoted to face the courtyard. When Azure stepped into it, the sunlight made her squint. The yard was large, and the ground had buckled in many places. Half a dozen were-dragons were gathered around a single figure in the middle of the courtyard. Oak crouched there with a long staff in his hands.

A weredragon wearing black armor, its orange wings extended, launched himself at Oak, who pivoted, deflecting the weredragon's assault easily. On the other side of him another weredragon hurled himself forward, but Oak ducked and the attacker flew over his head. The fight looked like it had been choreographed, and for that reason Azure simply stood and watched the strange dance. The weredragons all wore armor, some metal and others black leather. Each had the body of a man or a woman, although their skin was covered in iridescent scales and their backs were adorned with clawed wings of various colors. Their faces were more like Micky's, with sharp angles and horns protruding, and their eyes matched their wings and scales, making Azure wonder if each color was linked to a special ability.

A weredragon with bright-blue wings and scales caught Oak's staff and pushed him back with it, and where before the wizard's face had been focused now fear sprang into his eyes. Azure tensed, grabbing for her wand as Oak stumbled back weaponless. He halted when he'd been backed up to the stone wall. The bright-blue weredragon stalked forward, breaking the staff over his knee. The other weredragons just watched.

Azure lifted her wand. What should she do? If she attacked the weredragons to save Oak they'd never give her a scale, but she decided it didn't matter and pointed her wand. The bright-blue weredragon opened his mouth and roared. Ice shot from his lips, and he moved his face in a half-circle. Azure was trying to determine the best spell to use when laughter filled the courtyard, and the one laughing loudest was Oak. Around him on the wall was a line of ice and frost as if he'd been framed against the stone.

"It appears I'm no match. I guess I'm rusty from the new life," Oak said, pushing off the wall and smiling broadly.

"Valiant effort, my friend," the bright-blue weredragon said, nodding at Oak.

Azure lowered her wand. So it had been a game, of sorts—sparring practice. She relaxed her shoulders. Knowing Oak hadn't been in real danger was a giant relief and Azure released a breath, thinking that this was going to be a whole lot easier than she had thought.

She cleared her throat, and every weredragon in the courtyard swung around to face her. The bright-blue weredragon shot across the intervening space, halting only a few feet from her. Azure tensed at the sudden movements. The weredragon looming over Azure opened his mouth, his breath misting. "How dare you enter our sanctuary, human! Your death will be fast."

Azure stumbled back. "Wait, I only followed Oak in here. I'm Queen Azure—"

"I don't care if the officials allowed you to come to Lancothy. Trespassing here is punished," the weredragon snarled, his eyes narrowed with hostility.

"Hoarfrost, she's with me—the one I told you about," Oak interrupted. He attempted to stride over, but was prevented by the other weredragons.

"It doesn't matter. This is our home, and she shouldn't have entered. What if I just barged into your home?" Hoarfrost asked her.

"I'm sorry. Oak entered, though. I don't understand," Azure said.

"Oak is one of our brothers, and this is just as much his home as it is mine," Hoarfrost said.

"I'm sorry, I'll—"

Azure's words were cut off by something in her head— a voice like the one before.

Don't apologize. Dragons believe it shows weakness. Assert yourself.

Azure wondered if that was Micky. She straightened.

With Oak being restrained and Hoarfrost bearing down on her she had little choice.

"I meant to say that I'm here because I have business," Azure began, her voice clear and loud. "I'm the queen of Virgo, and the new protector of the Howling Willow. If you have a problem with the fact that I invited myself into your castle, maybe we *should* fight. I, however, think that's a horrible waste of time while vampires are spreading an epidemic and a zombie is loose in Lancothy."

Hoarfrost studied her with anger flaring in his eyes.

"None of that erases the fact that you have trespassed and spied on us," the weredragon said, frost on the edges of his lips.

Azure paged through possible replies. How could she not apologize? How could she show strength? She felt Micky somewhere in her mind, lending her a strength she'd never felt before. It felt as old as time, and felt like her connection to the Howling Willow. Azure drew in an unhurried breath. "Again I ask, do you wish to duel over this matter? I'm not your enemy, but if you persist then you'll make one of me."

Hoarfrost opened his mouth, and Azure tensed. She was bluffing so hard she thought a sign was printed on her forehead declaring it.

Quite suddenly, Hoarfrost bowed low and the were-dragons at his back knelt. When he straightened his face looked quite different, and he had a prideful appreciation in his eyes.

"You have my respect, Queen Azure. I took you as a cowardly witch, but now realize I judged you poorly." He

SARAH NOFFKE

indicated a giant room off to one side. "Please, will you join us? We will be dining soon."

Azure wanted to jump up and down. It had actually worked! She had been seconds from being frozen, but thanks to Micky she'd stood up to the weredragon and saved her ass. She nodded, holding her chin high. "Yes, I accept your invitation."

15

Monet and Ever strolled through the city of Lancothy trying to pretend that the glances they were receiving from the vendors they passed didn't indicate contempt. Monet had even chanced a jolly smile at a wereoctopus, which was why there was ink all down the front of his robes.

"Guess that will teach me to be friendly!" he remarked, pulling his wand from his robes.

Ever held up a hand to stop him. "Remember what Laurel said about using magic in Lancothy?"

"That the Weres have an inferiority complex, and would probably revolt against such things," Monet said with a sigh, putting his wand away again. He directed his voice to the stall where the wereoctopus was still seething. "Fine. I adore wearing octopus ink on my robes. It's a lovely pattern."

"Good job not attracting attention to us," Ever said through a laugh.

"Is it really my fault if my dynamic personality and stunning good looks attract attention?" Monet asked seriously.

"No, it's not. Such a curse you were born with, you sexy mofo," Ever said as they left the market area and passed into the city center. The main government building stood in the center of the square, the flag high on its steeple waving in the wind. The faces of a dozen animals could be seen on the rippling fabric, and engraved over the entryway were the words **Inside the Mountain we find Peace**.

Both men stopped and looked at the columns and the steps that led into Lancothy's courthouse. They were there to convince the officials to aid them in their battle against the vampires, but Ever felt there might be a bigger mission for him. The day had started with news that had tightened his heart, but he still believed things could be turned around. Maybe Ever would never have what he longed for, but why not try and give that to others even if they didn't know it was what they wanted? The people of Lancothy operated out of fear, meaning they merely survived. Ever thought he knew how to change things so that one day these wereanimals would thrive.

After Laurel made it to the top of the ladder, Blisters knocked her over because he was so excited to see her. He'd been afraid she'd fallen to her death, or that a wereeagle had snatched her. The bird might have carried Laurel to its nest, unbothered by her screaming and thrashing, and there she'd have been dinner for the wereeagle's four babies. That was just one of the many thoughts Blisters had entertained regarding Laurel's fate.

Overly excited by Laurel's survival of the possible wereeagle attack Blisters ran straight at her, nearly knocking her over the edge. Her nails scratched at the cliff as she scrambled back up. Manx, in raven form, had grabbed the back of her shirt in his beak and was using it to lift her.

"That's not helping," Laurel complained breathlessly. She finished her climb and set her back against the cave wall, winded. "You two are trying to kill me, aren't you?"

Blisters shook his head. His insides felt like pudding. Harming Laurel had not been his goal. In fact, that was his antigoal, but now he saw how in his excitement he'd put her into a dangerous position. He was always doing this kind of thing—wanting to help and then screwing it all up. It didn't matter that he was a unicorn with spectacular wings. He was causing more problems than helping.

"I'm sorry, Laurel. Truly sorry," Blisters said, backing up.

"Where are you going?" Manx asked, having changed into a goat.

"I'll go check out the cave for bats and leave you here, as far away from me as possible," Blisters whimpered, his voice hoarse.

"Blisters, I know you were just excited. It's okay," Laurel's voice called from behind him, but he had already made up his mind. He trotted into the dark, slick cave.

Azure shot a tentative look across the thick wooden table at Oak . The large room was stifling, as if they were inside the belly of a dragon. Azure peeled off her robes, throwing them over a chair before taking a seat.

She realized at once that sitting down might have been a bit presumptuous of her, since all the weredragons were waiting in front of their seats.

Azure shuffled to push out of her seat, but before she did she heard the voice in her head again. Micky's voice. *Own it. Make them think they should be waiting for you, not the other way around.*

Weredragon traditions and customs were so strange. Why hadn't Oak told her anything to prepare her for all of this?

Azure pushed her chest out, making eye contact with Hoarfrost. "You may all sit," she said, her voice not betraying the fear vibrating inside of her.

"Very well," Hoarfrost said, motioning to the seats.

To Azure's relief Oak took the seat next to her. He turned to fix his robes, whispering quietly so only she could hear it, "Well played, Queen. Continue to open your mind to Micky. It will keep you alive, and help our chances."

Azure nodded, but covered the gesture by raising a large goblet to her mouth. The water was hot, nearly burning her tongue.

"Oak tells us you want one of our scales," Hoarfrost said, which produced much laughter around the table.

"And he said that although you might give it to him, you won't give it to me," Azure agreed, sitting tall.

"That's correct," a green weredragon on the far side of

the table told her. "A family might be willing to give something valuable to a family member, but they will not offer it to someone outside the unit. Now, what the family member chooses to do with it…that's their business, especially if it will benefit him in return."

Azure nodded. That made sense.

"Since we know Oak doesn't want the scale for himself, it's important that we know who it goes to and why," Hoarfrost said.

"I have a genie in a lamp, and I want to release him," Azure said.

"I've never heard that our scales had anything to do with giving genies freedom," a red weredragon next to Azure said.

"That's right," she replied. "There's a witch in New Egypt who knows how to free the genie."

"And she wants the scale in return for the information," Hoarfrost guessed.

"Yes, so grilling me will not offer you what you want to know about where the scale will end up. Will that be a problem?" Azure asked, injecting confidence into her voice.

Hoarfrost and Oak exchanged looks. "Your mission is an honorable one, although you should know that if this witch uses the scale for something nefarious you will be liable."

If you agree to that they won't relinquish the scale to Oak. This is a test. Dragons love their games.

Azure ruminated on Micky's advice, then tapped her fingers on the surface of the table, looking at each of the weredragons briefly. "I refuse to be held responsible for what another person does. As you have mentioned, my reason for wanting the scale and my overall mission are honorable. How dare you expect me to pay the price for someone else? I wouldn't even do that for someone in my kingdom."

The weredragons rustled their wings as they exchanged curious glances. "You do not speak like most humans," Hoarfrost said.

"How would you know how humans speak? You have barricaded yourself inside of Lancothy for a long time. When did you last see a sunset?" Azure dared to ask.

"We do not need to see the sunset. We share our ancestor's memories and see the setting sun as they once did," Hoarfrost replied.

Azure gave a quiet laugh. "To dream of a sunset and to experience it are two very different things."

"You are quite bold, aren't you, witch?" Hoarfrost asked, his voice crackling with anger.

He can help you with your goal. Demand his help, Micky said in Azure's mind.

Azure drew in a breath that seemed to burn her nostrils. "Hoarfrost, the officials will be considering something radical very soon. Will you support the idea?"

"Why should I?" he asked, his voice sharp.

"Because you know I'm right," Azure began. "The memories of your ancestors will only sustain you for so long, and if you review them you'll realize there's little to fear. You are, after all, weredragons. I was under the impression that was something to be revered." Azure shrugged, peering downward as if she'd changed her mind.

"Maybe the rumors are false. Maybe weredragons aren't fierce after all."

Several of the weredragons emitted soft growls that echoed around the room, and their eyes glowed brightly as they leaned toward her. Azure pressed back into her chair, slipping her hand under the table to search for her wand. Many of the weredragons leaned forward as if they were about to pounce on her and she had a flash of being over-whelmed by the beasts, unable to combat their fire, ice, and who-knew-what-else. Would Oak be able to save her?

A large silver cart thundered through the door, yanking everyone's attention in that direction. Sitting on the cart, which was being pushed by a weredog, was a roasted pig, one of the animals from the farms on the far side of the valley. Behind the cart, a werecat carried a tray steaming with other roasted meats. The weredragons turned to the table, gnashing their teeth and uttering guttural growls.

"Dinner's timing has saved you," Hoarfrost said from across the table. "As for your demand, Queen Azure, we shall see."

A plethora of wereanimals were scattered down the long corridor of the government building. Monet pulled his hood over his head, partially covering his face. Some were-animals could change into human form, and some were stuck in-between. Many had regressed so far that they were mostly animal, having lost any trace of their human form. The ones in the building were like Laurel. They looked like animals, but exhibited the poise of humans as they conversed and walked. A weregiraffe and a werezebra stared Monet and Ever down as they passed.

"We've officially strolled into the belly of the beast," Monet said between tight lips. "But what kind of beast, I don't know. Maybe a hippo?"

"Leave the talking to me," Ever said, stopping in front of a reception desk. A weredeer pinned her eyes intently on the two as she waited for them to address her. She uncrossed her hooves on the surface of the desk and recrossed them the other way.

"What is your business here in Lancothy?" she asked.

Everyone in the hall halted to listen.

Ever straightened. "We represent the queen of Virgo. She has a meeting with the officials."

"Where is the queen, then?" the weredeer asked, looking behind Monet and Ever.

"She had business with the weredragons first," Ever answered.

The weredeer stood up from the desk. Her long body was covered in a black robe, the kind Laurel wore. "The queen set up a meeting with the officials, but she thinks it better to meet with the weredragons. Is that right?" She shook her head and clicked her tongue with disapproval.

"I'm sure they will understand that we are all pressed for time," Ever stated as the weredeer opened a door and ushered them inside.

"You know little if you think the officials will be so understanding," the weredeer told them.

"Blisters, you've saved Oriceran from vampires, found a potion to make Gillian grow, and discovered a plant that produces marshmallows. How can we ever thank you?" Blisters said, his voice squeaky. He trotted forward and then bowed slightly, enjoying his fantasy.

"Queen Azure, saving your kingdom is thanks enough for me. I do all this because I'm noble at heart," Blisters said, blinking up at an imaginary Azure.

"And then they'll throw a huge party to celebrate me," Blisters sang, spinning around, his eyes wide with excitement from his vision. "Witches will lavish me with garlands, and wizards will kneel to me when I prance through the streets. And dumb old Manx will have to clean up after me every single day."

Something scratched at the cave floor behind Blisters. He whipped around, expecting Manx to have followed him. Even squinting, though, it was hard for Blisters to make out anything. He'd traveled so far into the cave that there was little light. A glow showed in front of him, where the cave emptied into the valley.

Blisters desperately wished he'd paid more attention during his unicorn lessons. How many times had he said that, though? With the right level of concentration his horn could glow, which would offer him a little light, but the elders had given up trying to teach him the skill.

Blisters clamped his mouth shut, held his breath, and pushed all his efforts into making the horn on his head light up. Air shot out of his ears instead.

"Errrr…" he said, kicking at a nearby wall and slipping. His hooves scrambled underneath him a few times before he landed flat on his stomach.

Wet and frustrated, Blisters tried several times to get back to his feet, but only slid back down. He let out a long breath after he finally secured his balance.

"Chicka-chicka-chicka," something whispered at his back.

Blisters spun around, nearly falling again. "Manx, is that you?"

"Chickaaaaa," the voice whispered.

"This isn't funny," Blisters said. "How did you get on that side of the cave? I didn't see you pass me." The dumb pooka had probably flown over Blisters' head. He had to remember that he could fly now too. He shouldn't allow the pooka to get the better of him by putting snakes and spiders in his—well, Monet's—bed. When they returned to the House of Enchanted, Blisters was going to defend himself against Manx. Stand up for himself for the first time.

"Chicka...sssssss," the voice said.

Blisters froze. Blinked. He needed to see what was up ahead. He strained with all his might to make the horn light up, and a loud fart echoed through the cave.

"Oh, shoot," Blisters said, his cheeks warming with embarrassment. Whoever was ahead—or whatever—well, they weren't laughing at him, which was good.

"Hello?" Blisters asked. "Is someone here?"

Blisters felt something scuttle by him. Something large...nearly his size.

"Hello?" Blisters asked, pressing back against the wall, his heart hammering. "Who are you?"

"Scabs," something said, its voice deep.

Blisters shuffled forward. Maybe he'd just met a friend.

The light from the other side of the cave grew in intensity as he went in Laurel and Manx's direction.

"Scabs? I'm Blisters," he said.

"I know who you are," the voice said from in front of him. "I've been watching you." Scabs' voice was now behind him.

"Watching me? Why?" Blisters asked, turning around and blinking in the dark.

"Because I'm your shadow," Scabs said.

"Shadow?" Blisters laughed. "That's silly."

"Is it? Not if you're me, and tired of being left in the dark," Scabs hissed.

Blisters pushed power into his horn, focusing like he'd never done before. He felt the horn warm and then the faintest of glows blossomed between his eyes, bathing the area in a soft light—which was when he saw it. Standing only a few yards away was a unicorn just like him—the same size, and with wings and a glowing horn. But Scabs wasn't white with rainbow hair and blue eyes. Scabs was black. Entirely black, and he wore a sinister grin.

16

"Queen Azure," Hoarfrost said, pulling one of the closest platters of meat toward him, "All we have to serve you is meat. If that is a problem—"

"It's not a problem." Azure grabbed a drumstick from a roasted chicken in front of her. She bit straight into the meat, tearing through skin and gristle.

Hoarfrost watched her for a moment. Micky was obviously telepathic. Were the weredragons telepathic as well? She didn't think so, for some reason. Or maybe her mind was open to Micky and closed to these weredragons. Gran had said that telepathic links were sometimes automatically established when someone became a protector and was therefore trusted.

Beside Hoarfrost a weredragon with red scales and wings held up a giant chicken thigh. He opened his mouth and fire shot out, blackening the meat.

"It was cooked perfectly," the weredragon next to Azure said. She had yellow scales and more elegant wings than the others. "I'm not sure why you insist on burning your food, Inferno."

"I don't dictate how you eat *your* meat," Inferno replied, his red eyes narrowing. "Why do you think you can tell me how I should eat, Lightning?"

The weredragon didn't answer. turning instead to Azure, her eyes brimming with curiosity. "What does Oak want from you in return for the scale?"

Azure wiped the grease from her mouth with her fingers since napkins hadn't been provided. She could be a real pain in the ass and ask for one, but decided that she'd better play it safe since she hadn't been struck with fire, ice, lightning, or anything else just yet.

"How do you know he wants something in exchange for the scale?" Azure asked. Oak was deeply engaged in a conversation with the green weredragon on his other side.

Lightning smiled, showing deadly sharp teeth. "This world and all others are based on exchange. Nothing exists for long that does not take and give. It is the natural order of things."

Azure mused on this notion. "What about gifts? Maybe Oak is simply giving it to me."

The weredragon nodded. "Gifts are given with the intent of receiving something in exchange. Is that what he's doing? Usually it is affection, admiration, or good will. Is that the case? Is Oak giving it to you as a gift?"

Azure shook her head. "It's true that he's asked for something. He wants me to give him the essence of true love in exchange for the scale."

Lightning leaned forward, appraising Oak with admiration. "That warrior never gives up, I'll give him that much."

Azure turned to look at Oak, perplexed. He was still talking excitedly to the other weredragon and didn't seem to know he was the subject of the neighboring conversation. "You mean," Azure said to Lightning, "Oak has been trying to get this for a while?"

"I do not know Oak, nor do any of us," Lightning began. "However, we are connected through our ancestral consciousness, and that informed me long ago that Oak was on the hunt for the essence of true love."

Dragons were incredibly strange and wonderful creatures, Azure thought. They had such an interesting connection to one another, like how Micky was hooked into Azure's mind. Now that she was aware of the connection, she felt the dragon in her mind like a hook in fabric.

"If he's been trying for so long, I'm guessing securing it will be difficult," Azure said mostly to herself.

"I understand that true love—or any emotion, for that matter—is nearly impossible to contain. True love will probably be the most difficult," the weredragon said.

Azure set down her drumstick as doubt filled her insides, making her suddenly lose her appetite.

"Most don't know how to contain true love correctly and waste their chance, since it can only be caught when the emotion is first felt and therefore flaring strongly," Lightning said, her bright-yellow eyes intense. "But the real problem is that finding true love is incredibly difficult. Furthermore, being in the right place at the right time to capture the emotion is another impossible part of the equation."

Azure's face must have registered her defeat because

Lightning said, "This doesn't mean that it's impossible. Unlikely, maybe."

"It sounds like my first problem will be finding out how to contain the essence of true love," Azure said. She'd never heard of emotions being contained, and wished she would have asked Gran about it when she'd had a chance.

"That's where most fail, I suspect," Lightning said, eyeing Inferno with disgust as he blasted another piece of meat.

"Do you know how it's done?" Azure thought it would be a longshot to ask a weredragon for the solution, but she was more than desperate.

"I do not," she replied. "However, there is a witch named Dolly who knows."

Azure wondered how this weredragon who had never left Lancothy could know such a thing. *We're all connected*, Micky said in her mind.

Right, Azure thought. The dragons seemed to share a universal mind, which was akin to how she was connected to everything through the Howling Willow.

"Dolly…" Azure repeated. "Where do I find this witch?"

"I do not have an answer to that," Lightning said.

Azure nodded and thanked the weredragon for what she had offered, then excused herself from the table. She needed to get away from the blistering heat in the room and find some fresh air. Her head swam from the warmth, and the impossible task of finding a witch on Oriceran knowing only her name. Even the Howling Willow needed more than that to supply information.

"The officials will see you now," the weredeer said, pointing to a room at the end of the hallway.

"Did you bring a presentation, because I was just going to wing this whole thing?" Monet said to Ever. The young wizard was trying to lighten the mood, since he increasingly felt like they were walking into a trap. They'd ambled farther and farther into this stone building, earning contemptuous stares from all they passed. There was nothing stopping one of the wereanimals from attacking them and imprisoning them forever. Monet cringed at the idea of having to eat wereanimal food, since he was pretty certain the kitchen staff weren't required to wear hairnets.

"All we have to do is state the facts," Ever said, always the voice of reason.

"Facts. Sure," Monet said, sliding through the door into a surprisingly bright room. It was long, and lined with windows. Behind a table were three cantankerous faces. Wereturtles. The officials were all reptiles with hard shells. Their saggy green skin made them look especially old.

"I like the color of your shells," Monet said, striding forward and pointing to his hair, which was the same shade.

"Where is the queen of Virgo, and who are you?" the turtle on the left asked, taking an exceptionally long time to deliver the question.

"Queen Azure sent us, and asked that we make a request of your government," Ever said, once again at Monet's side.

"The queen of Virgo is in no position to make requests. We only allowed her entry because council rules required it," the middle turtle said.

"There's an epidemic of vampirism spreading through Oriceran," Ever told them. "We have reason to believe that vampires will be entering the caves of Lancothy to capture the bats that reside there."

"That is no concern of ours," the wereturtle on the right said.

"It should be," Monet exclaimed, "because if vampirism spreads, all your people...errr, animals could be bitten."

"We have no magic, and therefore cannot be changed," the first turtle said.

"No, but you can be bitten and die from the virus," Monet stated. "I've heard that it eats at your insides until internal bleeding swamps your organs, and then you die an excruciatingly painful death."

All three turtles sucked their heads into their shells, probably to hide from the thought of such an end.

"An epidemic of vampirism is a problem for all of us," Ever said calmly.

"Could a vampire even enter our land?" one turtle poked its head out to ask the others.

"They aren't living, so I assume they can," the middle one replied after deliberating for what seemed like an hour.

"We're trying to find a way to protect the bats or move them back to Earth where they came from," Ever cut in. "Until then, we need your help with guarding them. We're outnumbered, but you could help us."

"How can we help?" one of the officials asked.

"We need guards at both entrances of the cave," Ever explained.

"Impossible," the first turtle retorted. "That would

require one of our residents to leave Lancothy. That's forbidden."

"That's another part of the problem," Ever stated. "Vampires could enter Lancothy at night. Since the werewolves own the night, that presents a huge problem."

"What do you propose we do about that, Light Elf?" asked the turtle in the middle. They all looked exactly the same, down to the spectacles they wore on their pointed faces.

"It's fairly straight forward," Monet said. "The shaman who cursed Lancothy said that as long as the wereanimals cut themselves off from the rest of Oriceran this land would remain out of balance. Seems pretty simple to me."

The turtles ever so slowly looked at each other. "We're not following you," the one on the left said.

Monet suppressed the condescending sigh that was longing to spill from his mouth. "Open your borders. Leave Lancothy. Break your curse."

Loud gasps shot from the officials' mouths before their heads disappeared back into their shells.

"Oh, come on, guys!" Monet complained. "It's beautiful and bright out there in the world. You have no idea what you're missing."

"We know we're missing nothing," boomed a voice behind them. There was a giant werebear standing squarely in the entrance, his body entirely blocking the door.

Laurel gritted her teeth and hit two stones together, but

frustratingly it only produced a small spark. Again. For ten minutes she'd been trying to light the torch Manx had helped her make.

A commotion echoed down the tunnel and Laurel turned, squinting. She could see well in the dark but not well enough to locate all the bats, since the animals blended into the cave so well.

She registered Blisters speeding in their direction. The unicorn collided with her, knocking her down on her back. His hooves pressed sharply into her side as he tried to push his head under Laurel's body.

"Blisters, what's gotten into you?" Laurel asked, shoving him off her. She rubbed her arms, which the scared unicorn had nearly trampled. Thank goodness he wasn't that large, or they'd all be dead by now.

"Th-th-there's something in the cave," Blisters stuttered.

Laurel and Manx exchanged nervous glances. "Is it a vampire?" Manx asked. He was in his dog form.

Blisters shook his head, his rainbow mane swinging into his face. "No. It's a-a-a unicorn named 'Scabs.'"

Laurel couldn't help it. A laugh erupted from her mouth. It made her feel better that Manx joined her, laughing and barking at the same time.

"I'm serious, guys," Blisters said. "I saw him. He has black hair and a black mane, and his eyes were black. And get this…even his horn was black."

Manx abruptly stopped laughing and looked quite serious. "I have a question."

"Yes?" Blisters asked. "What?"

"What color were his hooves? Don't tell me they were black too?" Manx asked, overcome by more laughter.

"This is serious, guys. This unicorn said he was my shadow and h-h-he sort of growled at me. I have a feeling he wants to hurt me," Blisters said.

"Growled at you?" Manx asked. "Why didn't you say so before! That seems pretty serious."

"I told you it was," Blisters said breathlessly.

Manx turned to Laurel. "Sounds like you should go start a cat-fight. Hiss at that growling unicorn."

Laurel shook her head. "Blisters, we don't have time for these games. We're trying to start a fire so we can see the bats."

"Oh, was *that* why you were trying to start a fire, little kitty?" Manx said, laughing again.

"Yes, and you're the one who made the torch," Laurel said, pointing at the stick on the ground.

"My bad," Manx said. "I just thought you were cold." He shifted into his stallion form, which took up most of the space, his head nearly brushing the ceiling. His eyes shone like beacons, casting a pure white light.

"Are you kidding me, Manx?" Laurel asked. "You forgot to tell me that you had built-in lights?"

"Oops," Manx said, not at all sounding remorseful.

17

The damp air outside in the courtyard of the castle was a welcome change from the stuffy room where the weredragons sat devouring their meat. Azure thought about checking on Micky, but decided that she had better not draw attention to the dragon, who had stationed herself at the entrance of the castle. Micky seemed to know what she was doing.

Instead Azure took this rare moment alone to relax. Settling herself down on a bale of hay, she closed her eyes and listened to the rhythm of her breathing. Reynolds, when he was her tutor, had taught her about mini-meditations. The wizard had encouraged Azure to take timeouts to center her thoughts.

"If you can find a quiet space in your head, usually you'll find there are answers written there," Reynolds had once told her.

"I know where to find Dolly," a squeaky voice said in her head.

Wow, this meditation business is great, Azure thought. She had never found an answer so fast before. Usually she had to really settle into her practice.

"*Psst…* Did you hear me?" asked the voice again, tickling her ear.

Wait, it wasn't in her head. Azure opened her eyes to find the courtyard empty. She stared around, trying to find where the voice had come from.

Something zipped in front of her face.

Buzz. Buzz.

Azure swiped her hand through the air to swat the horsefly as she continued to try to find the source of the voice.

"Hey, stop it," the voice yelled. "I'm trying to help you, you ungrateful queen."

Azure halted and her eyes crossed as she homed in on what was buzzing just in front of her face, as she leaned back it came into focus. Floating in the air was a tiny man of sorts. He had giant pointy ears, whiskers like Laurel's, and was wearing a brown suit like Gillian's—but the strangest part was that the small man was riding a large horse fly. It hovered in place briefly before circling around and landing on the hay bale next to Azure.

"What are you?" Azure asked, scooting off the bale onto the ground so her chin was even with the small man and his fly. It had been outfitted with a harness, from which the man dismounted.

"I'm Pedgit, the brownie," the tiny man said, bowing slightly.

"Brownie?" Azure asked. She'd read about those—

mythical creatures who cleaned cottages in exchange for biscuits and honey. "I didn't think brownies were real."

Pedgit slapped the fly on its side, and it lifted into the air and flew away. "You just dined with hungry were-dragons and you're questioning my existence?"

Azure squinted at the man. He was about the size of a thimble, with rosy cheeks and disheveled hair under his lopsided cap. "Sorry, that doesn't make any sense. I just didn't know that brownies were... Well, I always thought you were fairytales."

Pedgit puffed out his chest. "Real, we are." He swept his arm at the courtyard. "Who do you think is responsible for the upkeep of this castle?"

"You are?" Azure asked.

"And a dozen other brownies, so I can't take all the credit. Lord knows they'll hear about it if I try." Pedgit settled onto his knees and began digging into the hay bale, looking for something.

"Oh, well, I'm sure the weredragons are really grateful for your help," Azure said, watching the strange little man.

Pedgit pulled his hand from the hay and shook his head. "They don't know we even exist. It's the brownie's job to serve and we do it without compliment or payment, although we might nick a bit of food and drink here and there."

"I'm sure that's a reasonable exchange," Azure said, watching as the brownie sank his hand into another spot in the hay bale.

"Where on Oriceran did I put that?" Pedgit asked, feeling around deep into the hay. "I know I stuffed some a Chianti in here."

"What are you looking for?" Azure asked.

Pedgit pulled out a small bottle, triumph on his face. "Here it is," he said, uncorking it and taking a long drink. "And I'm here because you're looking for something, or rather someone."

"Dolly, the witch," Azure guessed. "You heard that conversation?"

Pedgit nodded, hiccupping as he took another sip of red wine. "I did indeed."

"And you know where to find her?"

"I've cared for many homes across Oriceran and Earth in my time," Pedgit stated, sitting down and getting comfortable with his bottle. Azure thought she might sneeze from the hay, but held it in. One sneeze from this distance would probably end her new friendship forever.

"I'm most grateful for your help," Azure said, thinking that she'd finally gotten a lucky break. "Where can I find Dolly?"

"Las Vegas," the brownie chirped.

"Las-what?" Azure asked. "Where on Oriceran is that?"

"It isn't. It's on Earth." Pedgit drained the bottle and immediately got onto his hands and knees to dig into the hay bale again. He was teetering a bit by now.

"Oh," Azure said. "Where in Las—"

"Vegas. Las *Vegas*," Pedgit completed her sentence. "You'll find Dolly at the Graceland Wedding Chapel. That's where she works now, or did the last time I checked. I used to clean her house, but the desert air in Las Vegas was too dry for my skin so I returned to Oriceran."

"Graceland Wedding Chapel," Azure repeated, trying to

lock in the name of the place so she could remember it later.

"There it is." Pedgit pulled another full bottle of red wine from the inside of the hay bale. Who knew how many he had hidden in there—or elsewhere in the castle.

"This Dolly…she knows how to contain the essence of true love?" Azure asked.

"I'd think so," Pedgit said, spilling a bit down his front as he uncorked the wine. He leaned forward and looked around as if he were trying to ensure they weren't overheard. "She's a love expert."

"Just the person I need to see," Azure said, her thoughts crushed by a sudden flash of Ever.

Ever took several steps back at the sight of the giant werebear. The last time he'd met Lorde, who was the leader of a rebel group of wereanimals, the bear had tried to murder him and Azure.

"Lorde, we've got this under control," one of the turtles said.

The werebear thundered toward Ever and Monet. He stood at least nine feet tall, and wore leather armor that was tied together with wire. His teeth were bared.

"You cowards can handle nothing," Lorde boomed, blowing hot rank air over Ever and Monet and the turtles behind them.

To Ever's surprise Monet stepped forward, hand extended. "Monet Torrance at your service. I'm the Potions

Master for Virgo, and have a wide assortment of breath-refreshing formulas that you might find handy."

"Wizard, you don't belong here." Lorde picked Monet up by his robes, holding him high in the air.

Unflustered, Monet said, "Actually, the ones who don't belong here are all of you. If you left this mountain the werewolf problem would go away, we could guard the bats, and the world of Oriceran would open its arms wide to your uniqueness."

Lorde threw Monet toward the door, but he disappeared before he hit it and reappeared in front of Lorde. "That wasn't very nice. I'm trying to help you."

Lorde blinked down at the wizard, his eyes crossing. "How did you do that?"

"It's called 'magic,' but don't hurt your big dumb brain with it," Monet spat.

"Monet," Ever warned.

"How dare you?" Lorde reached forward for Monet again but he stepped to the side, so this time the bear grabbed Ever and held him above his head. Ever was just about to create a spell to disable his attacker when he slammed to the ground. Lorde was on his side, having been hit by something.

"Staying inside the mountain of Lancothy is no way to live," Monet lectured the wereanimals, pointing his wand at the werebear who was scrambling to get back up. Ropes sprang from Monet's wand and wrapped around Lorde's arms and ankles. Ever stood up and cast a disarming spell to make Lorde less resistant. When he was fully restrained, the three wereturtles joined them in front of the powerless werebear.

"This is quite unorthodox," one of the turtles said.

"You've been allowing Lorde to bully you," Ever stated, looking down at the officials.

"He's right that the world outside Lancothy will judge us harshly. He wants to wage war on anyone who is different from us," the first turtle said.

"And how does that make you any different from those who ostracize you?" Ever asked.

"That's why we have remained inside Lancothy. We're safe here. It's the right thing for all, because inside the mountain we are at peace," the second turtle said.

"It might be the safe thing to do, but no one can live a full life in Lancothy—not you, and not the werewolves. The only option is to leave, and liberate yourself from the restraints your ancestors imposed," Ever said, his voice getting more intense as he spoke.

"We've heard your request, but we cannot honor it," the third turtle said, shaking his head. "Our ways preserve us. They keep us safe."

"But when you live in a mountain, it only takes one eruption to blow everything up," Monet argued, a new intensity in his eyes.

Lorde fought against the spell, turning his head to the side with venom in his eyes. "Our ways have served us. We will not subject ourselves to the judgments of others—not without a war."

Ever shook his head. "What you all fail to see is that war is coming. And because you've either stuck your head in the sand or chosen violence as a solution, you'll be ill-prepared when the enemy strikes."

18

The flying horses landed gracefully inside the Precinct of Mut. Sari didn't take the hand that Reynolds offered when she dismounted. The truth was that flying all day and searching for the missing *Book of the Dead* pages had worn her out, but no way in hell was she going to show it.

"Sari, the sun is setting," Gillian said, striding over. He had nearly fallen to the ground when he got off his own mount. Blisters was a better size for Gillian, but the gnome had jumped at the chance to ride the mysterious winged horse.

Sari scrunched her nose at the gnome. "Dear Gillian, I'm old, but I'm not senile. I'm well aware that night is quickly approaching."

"Then you're aware that when night falls vampires come out," Gillian stated.

"What?" Sari asked, her tone dripping with sarcasm.

163

"These vampires you're referring to…they won't hurt us, will they?"

Gillian pulled off his bowler hat and wiped his brow with his handkerchief. "I'm just not sure this is worth the risk. We can continue searching tomorrow."

"We're already here. Last site for the day, I promise," Sari said. The three had been searching pyramids and other ancient New Egyptian sites all day. The truth that Sari was starting to worry that the lost pages were on Earth, which meant she wasn't going to be able to help Azure find them. The trip to the Precinct of Mut had taken longer than Sari had expected, and she knew that Gillian was right to be worried. As soon as the sun set, the desert would be crawling with vampires.

"Let's be fast," Reynolds said, striding for the Mut temple.

They left the Pegasi by the Sacred Lake, which was shaped like the letter "C" and surrounded by trees. It would provide a bit of relief for the animals, which had been flying for most of the day.

The Precinct of Mut was located next to Djoser's Pyramid, which would have to be searched as well. Sari shivered at the idea of entering another dusty old pyramid. They'd been in so many labyrinths of tunneled chambers that day; she was quite tired of trespassing on burial sites. She much preferred the open temples comprised of statues and columns.

"This temple is fitting for you," Reynolds said as they entered the stone structure.

"I'm certain you're trying to bait me by piquing my interest," Sari said, her voice flat.

Reynolds' long black robe billowed behind him as he strode past engraved columns that soared high into the sky. "That I am. Mut was the Mother Goddess, and was married to Amun Ra, the King of Gods."

"She was also mother to Khonsu, the god of the moon," Gillian said, disappearing behind a statue of a lion-headed goddess.

"Why is that important?" Gran asked, staring up at the statue of Sekhmet. Similar statues littered the temple.

"Because Khonsu sought to create balance with the vampires, so he created werewolves. They were to be the vampires' natural enemy, corralling them one night of the month during the full moon. A werewolf's bite is deadly to a vampire, you know," Gillian said, walking back around the statue.

"So Ra, the sun god, made it so that vampires could only go out at night? And then Khonsu decided that on one of those nights each month they'd be hunted by were-wolves?" Sari shook her head. "If I didn't loathe the monsters I'd feel sorry for them. They can't catch a break."

"Yes, the Egyptian gods worked hard to create limita-tions for the vampires," Gillian said, disappearing behind a column.

"If they hadn't, there would be no stopping vampires. They'd be too powerful. Then we'd have no magic left on Oriceran," Reynolds said.

"And now we're that much closer to protecting that magic," Gillian said, coming around the other side of the column holding a thick piece of parchment.

Sari's mouth popped open. "Is that…"

Gillian nodded. "Yes, it's one of the lost pages from the *Book of the Dead.*"

19

The beast caught his prey's smell as soon as she left the castle, and he left the carcass he'd been devouring. The zombie's hunger was strongest when he was stalking the girl. It owned him all the time now.

Wiping the blood off his chin, the zombie narrowed his eyes at the figures emerging from the castle. He hadn't dared enter the high-walled structure; the smell of the dragons had been a natural deterrent. Instead he'd waited. The girl wouldn't always be guarded, and when she was finally alone he'd strike, then end his own suffering by bringing her to his master.

The zombie sank his teeth back into the flesh of the animal he'd killed for one last bite before staggering after the three, although he kept his distance.

Azure's eyes watered from the candles burning on the table in front of them, which gave off wisps of smoke. Needless to say, she'd had her fill of smoke and heat for the day. And meat...

The inn where they were staying was run by a surprisingly nice family of weremice. They had treated the group differently than others in Lancothy, offering a level of hospitality that had worried Azure at first. When she'd been hesitant, the mother of the family, who had over a dozen children scurrying around, gave her a sympathetic smile.

"We are often treated poorly by our own people," the weremouse explained. "They think we're weak, especially the predators. That's why we prefer to keep to ourselves on the outskirts here."

It appeared that the hierarchy of the animal kingdom operated strongly in Lancothy. Strange that they locked themselves away from prejudice but kept it alive in their segregated population.

"They flat out said no?" Azure asked, staring at the salad in front of her. When the weremouse informed Azure they didn't serve meat and apologized, she quickly put any worries to rest. Salad was just fine.

"Well, I believe the wereturtles' exact words were, 'We've heard your request, but we cannot honor it,' which pretty much sounds like no to me," Monet told her, staring at his own salad like he was hoping it would turn into a thick steak.

Azure pushed up from the small table. The group was a bit cramped in the two-room cottage, but they'd be safe for the night—which all that mattered. Oak and the dragons were secure in the barn. Micky had looked back several times when Azure had departed for the house, but there was no room for the dragon in the cottage and she couldn't remain outside without provoking the were-wolves. This was a chance Azure had to take, and even Oak knew that.

She moved to the window that looked out over the rolling hills. "Why do they have to be so stubborn.? Without the officials' help we're not going to be able to guard the bats. Don't they see that their own fear will cause their downfall?"

"There's nothing to fear but fear itself," Ever said, watching Azure as she stalked back and forth in front of the window.

"That's good," Monet told him. "I'm totally stealing that line from you."

"You're not stealing it from me, you're stealing it from Franklin D. Roosevelt," Ever informed him.

Monet opened his mouth to ask a question, but he shook his head. "Another Earth thing, I'm assuming. If I were you, I'd just take credit for all this stuff. We wouldn't be the wiser."

Ever pursed his lips and shook his head. "I don't think that's a good idea. No legacy is so rich as honesty."

Azure liked those words and the way they were strung together. "Who said that?"

Ever turned and gave her a look of offense. "I just did, My Queen."

"I'm sorry," Azure said, with a slight smile. "I just figured…"

"Well, my point is that honesty is the best policy," Ever said.

"I like the way you put that, although I wholeheartedly disagree," Monet said.

Azure leaned over and picked up Finswick, who'd spent the day hunting men the size of thimbles. Most in the group hadn't believed him when he'd told the story, but Azure knew he wasn't lying.

"How many bats did you find?" Azure asked Laurel.

"A whole whopping three," Laurel said, massaging her back. She'd apparently taken a series of falls.

"There have to be more than that in those caves," Azure said, absentmindedly twirling her wand in her fingers.

"I'm sure there are," Manx said. He was in fox form, sitting on the wide window seat. "And we would have found them if someone hadn't distracted us with a tall tale about a shadow self that was trying to kill him."

"I wasn't lying," Blisters cried from his place in front of the fire. He looked more defeated than Azure had ever seen him, and he'd lost his usual perkiness. "You should have seen him. He was black, with a black mane and tail. His horn was even black. And his eyes were—"

"Black...yes, we get it," Manx said, cutting him off. "Unicorns come in all different colors, just like pookas."

"That's the thing. Unicorns aren't black," Blisters said.

"Yes, and I was lying. Pookas are *only* black. It's a rule," Manx said.

"But a rose of any other color would still smell as sweet," Ever said, leaning back in his seat and intertwining his hands behind his head.

"I'm not sure what roses have to do with anything," Monet said, pushing his untouched salad away.

They hadn't made nearly enough progress today. The bats weren't secure, the officials of Lancothy were unwilling to listen to reason, and a zombie was hunting Azure. She looked down at Finswick, seeing something in his hair. Gingerly she picked out a little piece of cloth that was tangled into his black and white fur. It was a hat... from a brownie.

"Ever, do you think you could take me to Las Vegas?" Azure asked.

He looked up at her, his forehead creasing. "You're in a mood to gamble and get an STD, huh?"

"What? And what?" Azure asked. "No, I was told that I could find a woman in Las Vegas who might be able to help me with the containing spell. I still need to capture the essence of true love for Oak."

Ever thought for a moment. "I guess we can go tonight. I could open a portal inside the cottage."

"Oh, no, you don't," Monet said, standing. "Are there cheese and meat in this Las Wegas place?"

An amused smile spread across Ever's mouth. "There are buffets of cheese, meat, and everything else you can dream of in Las Vegas."

"Then I'm going too. I'm famished from defeating werebears and tolerating slow-ass wereturtles," Monet said.

"And as a bonus, there be more room in this cramped cottage," Manx said, standing and morphing into his dog form.

Now was the time—she was away from the dragon. The zombie staggered across the grounds. The locks on the doors of the cottage couldn't keep him out. Nothing could.

The hunger overwhelmed him now, clawing at his insides, but soon it would be over. One bite—that was all it would take. Then he would carry the girl back to his master. He could walk through fire. Conquer any enemy. Completing his mission would give him the strength.

A howl ripped through the night but the zombie ignored it, having finally arrived at the thick wooden door of the cottage. He wrapped his gray fingers around the handle. His super-strength would aid him now. A pull or two and the lock would be no more.

The howling came again, closer now. Something sped past the zombie's back, and he swung around. The field was empty and dark...except for two red eyes.

"Argh," the zombie yelled, ambling away from the door. Nothing could keep him from his prey. He'd end this distraction swiftly.

Two more pairs of eyes blinked at him a few yards away. The werewolves stepped into the light cast by the cottage's windows and crouched, teeth bared, growling deep in their throats.

"Argh," the zombie roared, launching himself at the first werewolf. His hand went for the beast's eyes, his teeth for its throat. Nothing could hold him back, not even were-wolves, but at that moment the ground shook under his feet, knocking both him and the beast off-balance.

The other werewolves pounced on them and tore into

the zombie, who clawed at the monsters, kicking and punching even as they tore him limb from limb. The fight to stay whole was all the zombie could focus on, so he didn't realize that Lancothy was violently shaking, readying to implode.

20

Azure barely registered the ground shaking under her feet as she stepped through the portal holding hands with Monet and Ever. She spun around, but its light was already disappearing.

"What was that?" she asked the two guys.

"I'm not sure," Ever said, his face conveying his worry.

"Maybe it was nothing," Monet insisted, but he hadn't been there the last time they were in Lancothy. When they had attacked the werewolves, the mountain had begun to shake. It was a part of the curse—harm the werewolves and the mountain destroyed itself. The shaman had thought of everything.

"Let's just get what we came for and return as soon as possible," Azure said, heading toward a small building with a sign that read **Graceland Wedding Chapel**. She knew that opening portals wasn't easy, and returning to Lancothy before they had gotten what she needed would be a waste. Monet might be right, too. The shaking could have just been a result of opening the portal.

A woman with a beehive of gray hair greeted Azure when she entered the chapel. "Welcome, y'all. Blessed day, isn't it?"

A quick smile flicked to Azure's mouth. "Yes, it is. Excuse me, but we're—"

The woman ran her eyes over Ever and her smile widened. "Here to get married. You're in the right place. I'd put a ring on this one's finger too, if I were you."

Heat warmed Azure's cheeks. Shaking her head, she said, "No, we're not getting married. Actually—"

The woman's grin dropped. She took a quick glance at Monet and shook her head. "You two are getting married, then?"

"Fuck, no," Monet spat.

The woman nodded, relief on her face. "Yes, I didn't peg you two as a couple. Friends...that was my guess. And blue and green hair would never work together. Now blue and black, that's a fine match. I've found that—"

"Actually, we're in a hurry. We're looking for Dolly. Are you her?" Azure interrupted. She suspected the woman would go on and on about what physical traits worked best together for couples.

The woman tilted her head to the side. "Dolly? No, I'm not her. She's at her other job."

Great, now they had to go on a wild gremlin chase for this love expert.

"Where can we find her?" Ever asked.

"Dolly tends bar at Rick's," the woman said.

"Rick's?" Azure asked, thinking she ought to know this reference.

"Of course. You've got to check out Rick's Rollin' Smoke and Barbeque," the woman said, pointing in its general direction.

"Now we're talking. Drinks and meat," Monet said, looking at the ceiling, hands pressed together and gratitude on his face.

Azure thanked the woman and sped out the door.

"So Lost Vegas seems like my kind of place," Monet said as they found a spot at the crowded bar. Rick's was loud and filled with customers, many of them vying for the attention of the bartenders.

Azure discreetly pointed her wand under her robes at a woman tending bar. She had short black hair cut into a bob, and tattoos covering one arm. Unlike the coven's tattoos in New Egypt, hers were colorful and not comprised of ancient symbols. A gnome covered the top of one arm, and a giant heart with an arrow through it took up the other. She guessed this was her witch.

The woman spun around before Azure could place a summoning charm on her. "Oh, no! There will be no magic in *my* bar."

Azure had heard the woman, but most were too engaged in their conversations to have made out what she said. Sinking back an inch with an apologetic expression, Azure put her wand away. "I'm sorry. We're in a hurry. Are you Dolly?"

The woman strode over, tossing three cardboard coasters in front of them. "That I am, and you're a witch."

"Yes, and I need your help," Azure said, keeping her voice down.

"First, what can I get you and your Light Elf friend to drink?" the woman asked, her hand on her hip.

"Hey, what about me?" Monet asked, offended.

Dolly winked at him. "Oh, wizard, I already know what you want. Something strong. Coming right up."

"I think I'm in love," Monet said, leaning forward with a gooey look in his eyes.

"You wouldn't be the first. Bad boys fall for me faster than a Vegas wedding," Dolly said, turning over a glass and filling it with ice.

"We actually don't have time for a drink. Thank you, though," Azure said, her words rushed.

Dolly waved her off, filling two more glasses with ice. "You always have time for a drink, and by the looks of it you need one. I'll get you three of our specials while you talk."

"This is my dream girl," Monet said, elbowing Azure in the side.

"Pedgit, the brownie who used to clean your house, sent me to you," Azure began.

Dolly looked up from the shaker she was filling with various types of alcohol. "Brownie? I had one of those lovely creatures to thank for my tidy house?"

"Yes," Azure said quickly, "but he said the desert didn't agree with him."

"So that's why my place is messier these days. I thought it was just that my current old man is a pig," Dolly said with a laugh. As she shook the ingredients, Azure noticed more tattoos on the underside of her arm. A list of names, it appeared, but most were crossed out.

"Sounds like you need to ditch that ham and get with a real wizard," Monet said, leaning forward on the bar.

"Honey, I would, but I'd only break your heart," Dolly said, pouring the drinks.

"That works, because I don't have one," Monet said.

Azure bumped her shoulder into him, taking back the conversation. "Pedgit said you were a love expert and could tell me how to contain the essence of true love."

Dolly garnished the drinks with an orange peel and a cherry before sliding one in front of each of them. "That little rascal knew me well, didn't he?"

Azure, not wanting to be rude, took a quick sip of the drink. "*Damn*, that's good," she said.

"'The Old Man,'" Dolly said, nodding in agreement.

"Huh?" Azure asked, taking another sip. Dolly was right…Azure was overdue for a drink.

"That's the name of the drink," Dolly informed her.

"Can you help us?" Ever asked, wiping his mouth after taking a drink.

Dolly paused, seeming to consider the request. "Let me guess. Is it a dragon-tamer who wants this essence of true love?"

"How did you know?" Azure asked.

Dolly laughed. "It's always a dragon-tamer. And yes, I can help you with the containment device. I'll even tell you where the most potent place to capture true love is. However, finding it will be your problem. It's not easy, and hasn't been done successfully in a hundred years."

"How do you know that?" Monet asked, having finished his drink.

"Honey, I'm the love expert. When true love happens, I know about it," Dolly said, shaking her head.

"Containment device? Do I have to track one of those down now?" Azure asked.

"I actually have one. I keep it on hand for just such occasions. I work at the chapel in hopes of capturing true love, but strangely most of the couples that come in are simply infatuated with each other."

"So the couples who get married at the chapel aren't in love?" Ever asked.

"Maybe they are, but it's not *true* love," Dolly said, making another round of drinks. "The majority of people don't realize that true love is so rare that most never feel it. That's what makes it so valuable. I've been around for centuries and I've never experienced it, but Merlin knows I keep trying." She nodded to the list of names on her arm.

"Are those all men you've loved?" Azure dared to ask.

Dolly shook her head. "Heavens, no. These are the men I've married. I loved the first one, which was why I tattooed his name on my arm."

Azure read the top name. "Keith." The name was written in flowery black cursive, and had been crossed out with red ink. Under that name were six others, all of them crossed out except for the last.

"What happened to Keith?" Monet asked.

"He cheated on me with a siren, but the joke was on him because she was only using him to get a ride to Reno." Dolly poured the three another round of drinks.

"So that's why his name is crossed out," Ever guessed.

Dolly nodded. "Yes, and then Jeric came along and we got hitched. Well, I kind of had to put his name on my arm too, but as you can see, that didn't work out either." She pointed to the list on her arm, indicating Jeric's crossed-out name. "By then I'd set the precedent, and now each man I marry expects to get his name on the list. Let's hope that Andrew is different than the rest."

Azure leaned forward to read the last name on the list. "Andrew."

"I hope that it works out," Azure said.

"I don't," Monet spat.

"Anyway, you said you've got a containment device. May I please have it? I really need to try and capture true love," Azure said.

Dolly looked at Ever and then Azure. "Yes, and you just might. The heavens aren't really clear if it's in your future."

"A genie's life depends on it," Azure said quickly.

"Not to mention that it would bring great fortune to your dragon-tamer friend," Dolly said, holding out her hand palm up. She looked around before conjuring a black velvet ring box.

"Is that the containment device?" Azure asked.

"Yes," Dolly said, popping the box open with her other hand. It was, surprisingly, empty. Azure had expected to find an engagement ring in it for some reason. "When you come across two people who are falling into true love—and hopefully you catch it when the emotion is at its highest intensity or it won't work—you open the box. The emotion will flow into it, and when you shut the box the essence is preserved."

"Wow, that's especially easy," Azure said, having believed that it would take an incredibly complex spell.

"The most complicated things in life are especially easy when we use the right tools," Dolly explained.

"Like math," Monet said, draining his second drink.

"Like love." Dolly handed the box to Azure. "When we understand our own heart it is easy to fall in love." The bartender shrugged, melancholy on her face. "I guess I have more work to do to know my own heart."

Azure smiled sympathetically at the woman. "I think we all do."

"You said you could tell us where to find true love," Ever reminded her, his voice suddenly tight.

"Actually, I said I could tell you where the most potent place to capture true love is located. You'll have to find true love on your own." Dolly laughed.

"Right, that was what I meant," Ever stated.

"It is said that more people fall in love in this place than any other, so it would be a good place to hunt for the essence of this emotion," Dolly stated.

"My bedroom?" Monet asked, mock seriousness on his face.

Dolly didn't laugh. "I've heard more than one complaint about you in the bedroom, Monet Torrance."

Monet sucked in a shocked breath. "That's blasphemy."

Azure laughed. "I can believe it. Dolly, we really need to get back. Can you please tell us where this place is?"

"Of course, Queen Azure. It's the most romantic place on Earth." Dolly smiled, a hopeful spark in her eyes. "The Eiffel Tower."

21

Lux and Devo had been in the cave that led to Lancothy for only a couple of minutes when the ground began to shake under their feet.

Devo spun to Lux with fear in his small eyes. "Is this from our trespassing?"

"I have no idea," Lux said rudely. How was he supposed to know anything about this dumb land with its freak animals? They hadn't even known where to find the mountain. He was weary and frustrated from searching and living in caves. And if he had to feast on another woodland creature he was going to puke. They hadn't encountered any people in days.

The pair stumbled through the dark cave as rocks rained down on them. Lux was not an educated man, neither now nor in his mortal days, but he knew that hanging out in a cave during a quake was a bad idea. Something about the thing collapsing seemed to occur to him.

Shrieks rang out from overhead and Devo, who was in

the lead, ducked as a barrage of wings flapped in their direction.

"Those are the bats!" Lux yelled. "Don't duck, idiot. Catch them! That's why we're here."

"Right," Devo said, covering his head with one hand and waving the other through the air dumbly.

An avalanche of rocks began and the light from the cave opening behind them disappeared, casting them in blackness. That didn't matter since they could see just as well in the dark, but that had been their exit.

"Fuck! We're trapped," Lux said, spinning toward the exit.

"We'll just have to find another way out of Lancothy," Devo said, panting heavily.

"No shit!" Lux exclaimed. "But first we have to get those damn bats."

As soon as he said this the colony of bats turned, racing back in their direction. The avalanche was going to work in their favor.

"Grab the bags," Lux said, pulling his knapsack from his pocket. It wasn't an ordinary bag, but one enchanted by Ata to hold living creatures without killing them. It also remained small and easy to carry no matter how many items it held.

Devo swirled his bag through the air like a net, trying to catch bats as they flew overhead. Lux did the same, but had to jump to reach them. The bats squeaked, their wings beating air onto the vampires.

A moment later the colony had disappeared to the other side of the cave.

"Did you get any?" Lux asked, staring down into his

bag. Three. He'd caught three fucking bats. That was unacceptable. Cordelia and Hamilton would punish them if they returned with less than a dozen. They had big plans, and it involved creating a strong brood of Founder vampires.

"I think I got one," Devo said lamely.

"Come on. We need to catch more," Lux said, sprinting after the bats as the cave continued to rumble around them. They would have been only a blur to average eyes. The cave ended abruptly, and Lux nearly ran over the side of the cliff. He halted on the ledge and looked out over the strangest sight he'd ever seen. Lancothy was a sprawling kingdom with buildings and farms, all contained inside a mountain. The bats streaked past them, making patterns in the air as they flew away.

"Let's get them," Lux said, taking a few steps back and readying himself to launch.

"Wait," Devo said, extending a cautionary hand. "Do you think it's safe? There's a quake going on, and we don't know what's down there."

"There's bats down there, and that's what we came for. And we have to find a way out of this mountain. A dumb quake can't hurt us. Nothing can, remember? We're immortal," Lux said, and leapt off the cliff. He landed gracefully on the ground below as a howl pierced the air.

The ground shook so violently that Azure fell hard against the stone wall of the cottage after stepping through the portal. Ever and Monet fell after they stumbled through as well. Azure braced herself against the wall—which was splitting—as small rocks and mortar showered her from overhead.

Thinking hard as her teeth clanged together, Azure surveyed the small room. Laurel had Blisters under one arm and Finswick and Manx in the other.

"What's happening?" Azure asked, her voice vibrating from the tremors.

"The werewolves," Laurel shouted. "Someone must have harmed them worse than before."

I knew it, Azure thought.

The rafters cracked, and the walls of the cottage shook more violently.

"We have to get out of here," Ever declared. He dove at Azure, grabbing her around the shoulders and shielding her with his body. Going out into the fields with hungry and savage werewolves was not advisable, but staying inside the cottage, which was about to cave in on them, would be a death sentence.

Azure covered her head and darted forward to grab the door handle, afraid of what she'd find on the other side. Werewolves? A zombie? More destruction, in any case. Bracing herself, she wrenched the door open. She was beyond shocked at what she found on the doorstep.

22

Ata let out a relieved sigh as he stepped away from the cauldron, which was filled with bubbling scrying potion.

"What is it?" Nenet asked, sitting stoically in the far corner of the room he'd constructed as his potions lab.

"The zombie has been destroyed," he said, waving his crook over the surface of the cauldron.

"Then Queen Azure is safe for a little while longer," Nenet said, lightness in her voice. She'd been slipping away lately, and Ata knew it. Even though he supplied her with his blood, he couldn't save her morale. They had each other, but that wasn't enough. They needed their people, and their people needed their king. Ata might have been a prisoner, but Nenet had lost her humanity.

He saw the urges course through her, making her soft eyes turn wicked without her consent. As a follower, she was under the emotional and cognitive control of Cordelia and Hamilton. Whereas they only controlled Ata's actions, they controlled almost all of Nenet's consciousness. At least he could think and feel for himself. She was losing that, and soon she'd be lost and he wouldn't be able to save her. He didn't even know if salvation was an option for either of them, but he wanted to hold onto hope. It was all he had left.

"Queen Azure is safe from my zombie, but she has many other problems," Ata said, closing his eyes tightly. He'd been watching Azure as often as he could bear. When she had entered the Sphinx, it had been difficult for him to observe her confrontation with Chibale. His arrogance had almost made Ata crack with anger, but at the end his brother had confessed his crime and now appeared committed to finding Ata and helping him.

Hope was all he had. Hope that his brother would change his ways. Hope in a young queen who was fighting a war that should have been his.

"Will the queen make it out of Lancothy?" Nenet asked, still clinging to the shadows as if afraid to step into any light.

Ata opened his eyes and shook his head. "That I don't know. The mountain is crumbling. If she doesn't get out soon, she'll be trapped there forever and she'll most likely die. Everyone in Lancothy will."

"I used to think that death was the worst possible thing that could happen to me," Nenet said, her voice flat.

"Then you died, and realized that…" Ata and Nenet had been having these philosophical conversations more and more. It helped them both to hold onto what they had probably lost but were unwilling to admit they had.

"I realized that living without my humanity was worse," Nenet said.

"And your magic? Do you miss it?" Ata asked.

"Not as much as I miss my sister. I would happily give up my magic to see Nefertiti for a final time," Nenet said.

"You never got to say goodbye, which makes it worse," Ata said, staring at the surface of the cauldron but blind to anything but the visions in his head.

Nenet's chin lifted suddenly. "Cordelia and Hamilton are leaving."

Ata nodded. "I gave them the location of one of the pages from the *Book of the Dead.*"

"Once they have those pages they'll be unstoppable," Nenet said in a tight whisper.

"That's true, but I think you mean 'if' they get those pages," Ata said, waving his crook over the surface of the cauldron to conjure a different image.

"What do you mean? You gave them the location," Nenet said, running her tongue over her top teeth to feel her pointy fangs. She did that often, simultaneously intrigued and repulsed by the change to her mouth.

"I was ordered to find a location for one of the pages, and I did as I was told. However, I might have stalled in finding it, which could give others a chance to discover the page first." Ata stared down at the cauldron, a ghost of a smile forming on his face at the image of an old witch, a red-haired wizard, and a gnome reviewing the missing page from the *Book of the Dead.*

Nenet suddenly stood. "Ata, are you able to resist their orders?"

He shook his head. "Not really. I must still do as

Cordelia and Hamilton command, but I have found that the pace at which I complete the task is still subject to my will. I took my time finding the location of the lost page."

"That's something, at least. You're getting back some of your power against them," Nenet said, striding over. She paused, looking at the image on the surface of the cauldron.

Ata drew in a breath, hope warming his chest. "Let's just hope that these three from Virgo can find all the missing pages quickly. I can only stall for so long."

23

S tanding squarely in front of the door of the cottage, blocking all else, was Micky. Azure's mouth dropped open. She couldn't fathom why the dragon was there.

"Mademoiselle," Oak called, striding around Micky with a harried look on his face. "The time has come. Micky is ready to take you.

"Take me where?" Azure had to scream over the shaking, grinding, and mayhem all around them as Lancothy continued to crack and split.

"To the weredragon castle, of course," Oak said, pulling the reins attached to the bridle on Micky's face.

"But, Lancothy! I need to…" Azure had no idea what she had to do, which was exactly the problem. The mountain was destroying itself. It was nighttime, and the deadly werewolves were on the prowl. As queen she was supposed to know what to do, or so she thought. Quick and efficient decision-making was the sign of a good ruler, but just then she was clueless.

"You asked the weredragons to help you when the time came, remember?" Oak asked, pulling up Azure's hand and placing the reins in it.

"Yes, but that's because Micky told me to," Azure admitted.

"And you can hear the dragon in your mind, which means you're connected to your deepest intuition. That's where Micky's inspiration comes from—an intuition as old as the dragons," Oak said.

"So I need to go to the weredragon castle...and what? Ask for their help?" Azure asked, looking back at Ever and Monet, who stood just behind her.

"The weredragons have powers that other wereanimals don't. This mountain will not remain standing for long," Oak explained.

"The weredragons can help us get out of here, can't they?" Azure asked Oak, but it was the voice in her head that answered.

Yes, but time is running out, Micky said.

Azure nodded, turning to face the group at her back. "Monet and Ever, we have to get the wereanimals ready to evacuate. Gather them. Protect them. And bring them to the northern side of the mountain."

"They won't want to leave, even if their home is crumbling," Ever stated.

"That's why I need you to make them see this clearly. It wasn't our coming here that brought this destruction upon them. It would always have happened. No one can live in isolation forever. Something will always break if we set ourselves apart from others on Oriceran," Azure stated. She felt like the words weren't her own, and then she realized they weren't. The Howling Willow was speaking through her, and instinctively she knew it wouldn't be the last time.

"Don't worry, we'll get the wereanimals there," Monet said with strong conviction in his voice.

"That's not what worries me. It's the damn werewolves," Azure said, her throat suddenly dry as chalk.

"I will try to help with that," Oak said at Azure's side. "The other three dragons can serve as a distraction."

"But the werewolves! If we harm them—"

"The mountain will destroy itself," Monet finished. "Yeah, I think it's a bit too late for that. Whatever happened to the werewolves tonight looks to be irreversible."

"Because when an eruption starts there's no stopping it," Ever stated.

"Okay, yes, Oak. We could use your help with the werewolves. Thank you," Azure said, her heart beating fast from the constant tremors and the pressure of the moment. She looked down at Manx, who was in goat form. "Can you help with the bats? I don't know where they are, but we need to ensure they don't get out of Lancothy."

Azure didn't like the idea of trapping the bats in the mountain, but she couldn't allow a colony of bats to invade Oriceran. It would escalate the vampire epidemic, which was exactly what Cordelia and Hamilton wanted.

Manx morphed into a raven and lifted into the air. "You can count on me, Queen." He flew through the dark sky and disappeared into the night.

"What about me?" Laurel asked, her eyes wide with shock but also filled with her unyielding courage.

Azure knelt and picked up Finswick, then handed him

to Laurel. "Get your people and my oldest companion to safety, please." She added weight to the last bit.

Laurel didn't say anything, just nodded confidently.

"Okay, we all have our jobs. Be careful and swift, all of you," Azure said, fixing the reins of the dragon who had patiently waited at her side into her hand. She scanned the faces in front of her one last time before mounting the dragon.

"Azure," Monet said, looking up at her.

She merely gazed at him in reply.

"If anything happens, don't hesitate to use your last wish to save yourself. I know you want to save Bob, but selfishly, I would rather not lose you," said her best friend, a tender pain in his green eyes.

Azure nodded. "Hopefully it won't come to that."

"Hopefully," he agreed as Micky gracefully turned around, extended her wings, and launched herself into the air.

24

"How are we supposed to catch them?" Devo asked, looking at the bats who were swarming in the air, seemingly unnerved by the mountain crumbling around them.

That was a good question, and not one Lux had an answer for. "Maybe we can bait them."

"What do bats like?" Devo asked.

Lux rolled his eyes at his idiot partner. "Blood, dumbass."

"Oh, I thought they ate fruit," Devo said.

Lux shook his head. He'd be better off doing this on his own. He sank his fangs into his wrist and the blood flowed immediately, running over his lips and down his arm. He held up his wrist, waving it in the air. "Come and get it, you little rodents."

"Good idea." Devo followed suit.

The bats paused in midair as the smell of blood registered, then dove in Lux's directions. It had seemed like a good idea until he realized he was about to be mauled by hundreds of hungry bats.

He darted behind Devo. The larger vampire made a good shield for him. Bats streaked toward them and dove right at the two men. Devo was knocked over by the first rush, but Lux managed to capture a dozen or more. He could also thank the assholes for tearing at his flesh as they flew by. He waved his arms and snarled, fangs exposed, at the bats that were about to make another assault.

Lux sprinted over and pulled Devo up by the back of his shirt. He'd sustained multiple injuries.

The ground shook so violently that it nearly knocked them down.

"We have to get out of here. This thing is gonna blow," Lux said, staring at the town. Buildings were bouncing off the ground, their roofs splitting and walls crumbling when they hit.

Devo looked up and nodded his bloody face. "Yes, let's see if we can find a way out over there." He pointed to the northern side of the mountain.

Lux nodded and sprinted in that direction and the bats followed them.

Micky rose into the air, beating her giant wings rhythmically. Azure leaned close to her neck, careful to keep her face away from the sharp spikes. She tightened her legs around Micky's body after she dared to look down. Lancothy was stretched below her, and the devastation was evident. Azure found it hard to breathe, but didn't know if it was the higher attitude or the sight of the fires and destruction on the ground.

The weredragons' castle seemed almost untouched by the destruction. It shook, but appeared not to be as affected as the other buildings. Micky's back legs reached forward and she raised her head as she prepared to land. Azure tightened her grip on the reins when the weredragons rose from the center courtyard of the castle. They hovered, most of them looking up at the hole in the top of the mountain.

Azure yanked hard on the reins to slow her dragon. Micky, who had been focused on the landing, spotted the half-dozen or so weredragons and straightened out.

The weredragons headed for the hole.

"We need your help!" Azure yelled when she was close enough to the weredragons that they could hear her.

Hoarfrost and Lightning slowed, jerking their heads in Azure's direction, and shock sprang to the bright-blue weredragon's face.

"Witch, why does that dragon allow you to ride her?" Hoarfrost asked.

"I'm not sure, but we don't have time for that," Azure roared over the swift beating of wings. The other weredragons had halted their progress and hovered a little higher than Hoarfrost and Lightning.

"It appears that you've gotten your wish. Lancothy will soon be no more," Hoarfrost said, his voice neutral.

"This was not the way I wanted it to go," Azure spat, anger flushing her face.

"We don't blame you, Queen of Virgo, especially now that we see you have earned the respect of a dragon,"

Lightning said. "The truth is, we knew this day was coming. We're ready to make our home somewhere else—somewhere we can spread our wings."

"Your people need your help, though," Azure yelled, throwing her arm at the town and buildings littering the rolling hills.

"*These* are my people," Hoarfrost said, motioning to the other weredragons, who circled back down to join the conversation.

"You are a wereanimal," Azure argued. "The people of Lancothy are a part of your tribe."

"Do you not see that we reside in a high castle in this land? We may be *of* our people, but we're not *like* them."

Azure shook her head. "That's ridiculous. Only they can understand what it takes to be both human and animal. How can you desert them? Most can't fly to safety. Will you really leave them trapped in this mountain without a way to escape?"

Hoarfrost looked at Lightning and a strange silent communication passed between the two.

"I asked for your help when the time came, and that time is now," Azure said. As she spoke something rumbled overhead, and Azure ducked instinctively as dirt and rock rained down on them.

"What do you expect us to do?" Lightning asked.

"You have many powers at your disposal. Can't you use one of them to break through the mountain and clear a path for the rest of Lancothy to get out?" Azure asked.

Hoarfrost shook his head. "None of us have a power that could do that."

They could do it collectively, Micky stated in Azure's head.

The dragon rose higher, so that Azure was looking down on the weredragons.

"Do you have the power to break through the mountain if you work together?" Azure asked.

Lightning's expression shifted to awe. "We do, but it hasn't been used in centuries—not since Lancothy was first formed. It was the weredragons who hollowed out the mountain at the request of the werewolves," she stated in a low voice, like she was remembering this all.

"Then it would make sense that the power that created your home centuries ago can free your people from their prison now," Azure stated.

Hoarfrost rose so he was even with Micky and regarded Azure for a long moment. The sounds of destruction echoing through the mountain were a constant reminder of the chaos around them. "Dragons put great emphasis on the cycle of life. It is our nature. What we begin, we must end. You have given us an insight we might have missed. Queen Azure, you impressed us before with your bravery, and now you have inspired us with your wisdom." Hoarfrost glanced at the other weredragons before returning his gaze to Azure. "We will do as you have requested, Queen of Virgo. We will create a path to freedom."

Ever and Monet rushed over the grassy hills towards the city's center. The dragon streaked above them, and the Light Elf glanced over his shoulder at the figures flying in the opposite direction.

"Never thought I'd see the day that Azure rode off on a dragon when all hell was breaking loose," Monet said as they ran.

"I'm not sure I've seen *anyone* ride a dragon before," Ever agreed. "It's quite rare for them to allow such a thing. Oak is the first dragon-tamer I've ever met."

"Yes, Azure is a fearless warrior, queen, protector of the Howling Willow, and has a way with animals. What's not to love?" Monet asked, a sly grin on his face.

"She's quite impressive," Ever said, not breathless from the run.

"And yet none of those attributes define why you're obsessed with her." Monet leapt over a giant crack. The land was more damaged near the city center.

"I'm not obsessed," Ever declared.

"No, I guess you're not," Monet said as they neared the government building. Everyone was still in their homes, even though the mountain shook violently. They were too afraid to venture out while the werewolves roamed. Were they all willing to bury their heads and be buried by the mountain?

"I'm simply enamored of the queen. Who wouldn't be?" Ever asked. He'd never met anyone quite like her; he was certain that it was because she was a one-of-a-kind miracle. There couldn't be another Azure Vladar, not in a million years. Since the beginning he'd kept trying to find a flaw in all her beauties. He had shamed himself for searching for her shortcomings, but he just had to find one. It was the only way—the only way not to fall over a cliff, headed for an undulant ocean that would swallow him.

"I've known Azure most of my life, and I can tell you

that everyone is *enamored* of her," Monet said, halting right in front of the government building. He turned to Ever with a smirk. "But you, my friend, are absolutely in love with that woman."

Monet allowed himself a moment to observe Ever's embarrassment before turning back to the building. How uncomfortable it must have been to think you'd hidden your attraction, only to be called out on it? From a distance Monet had watched the Light Elf fall harder and harder, and he was way past the point of enamored.

As Ever tended to do, he deflected. "Where are we going?"

Slick move, Monet thought. "You're changing the subject."

"The mountain is about to implode!" Ever yelled as they ran into the building and across the smooth floor of the lobby.

Monet turned and took the stairwell up. "Yeah, yeah, whatever. And if you had been paying attention, you would have known where we needed to go to find the officials."

"Well, where are they?" Ever asked, taking the landing behind Monet.

"Exactly where you'd expect cowards to be when their kingdom is crumbling," Monet said, bursting up the last set of stairs.

"Hiding?" Ever guessed.

"No, watching powerlessly and doing abso-fucking-lutely nothing about it." Monet threw open the door to the roof and stormed out, halting when he was only five yards from the three wereturtles. They stood at the edge of the building, helplessly watching the city burn and rock around them.

"Are you just going to watch as your kingdom falls to pieces?" Ever asked them.

"There's nothing we can do," the first wereturtle called.

"You can evacuate your people," Monet said.

"There's no way we could get them through the caves or down the chute in time," the second wereturtle said, retracting his head into his shell.

"The queen is working on a way to get everyone out. We need you to order the wereanimals to the northern side of the mountain," Ever said, his words tumbling out in a rush.

"It won't work. There's no way to get the message out. We're doomed," the third wereturtle cried.

"Oh, for fuck sake, will you stop acting like we're all going to die?" Monet pulled his wand from his robe, enchanting it with a broadcasting spell. He tried to hand it to the first wereturtle, but he jumped back like it was poisonous.

"Come on, you've got to make an announcement," Ever said. "Tell the people of Lancothy that they can be saved, but they're going to have to go out into the night. We'll do our best to protect them from the werewolves, but they have to come out."

"Most won't want to leave Lancothy," the second wereturtle said.

"They will do what you tell them to," Monet said. "They've always followed a leader. When they were told to bury themselves in this mountain, they did it. Tell them to leave, and they will. Tell them they're safe, and they'll believe it."

Oak's carriage streaked through the sky, pulled by two of his dragons. The wereturtles watched the carriage's progress over the sprawling city, which vibrated continuously now.

The third wereturtle reached for the wand, clearing his throat.

"We won't leave!" a voice boomed behind them.

Lorde thundered through the stairwell door behind Ever and Monet and barreled toward them.

Ever held up a hand to halt the wereanimal. Symbols lit up on his arms and hands as he whispered inaudible words and Lorde slowed, looking as though he were moving through quicksand. He gritted his teeth and kept his fanatic eyes on the group in front of him, still pushing forward.

"Our ancestors put us in Lancothy for a reason," Lorde said. "Outside these walls are devils who will persecute us for our differences. You may choose to forget what the history books say, but I won't."

"Things have changed in a thousand years," Monet said, wishing he had his wand in his hand. Ever was holding Lorde off, but only barely and not for long.

"Things will *never* change. Those outside Lancothy will never look at us as equals. If we leave this mountain, we will have war. We will have to revolt against the world that made us choose to imprison ourselves," Lorde boomed. He was making real progress now.

"You will not," Monet said defiantly.

"Lorde, we cannot choose to make war on a world we no longer know," the wereturtle holding the wand said.

"We are wereanimals! The world is our enemy." Lorde spread his arms wide before beating his chest, a thundering roar spilling out over his large canines.

"Then the world you shall not meet," Ever stated. He pulled his hand to his chest and then thrust it forward hard, throwing Lorde back several yards as a large shadow cast them in darkness.

The dragons had pulled the carriage overhead and now opened their mouths, shooting fire at the crazed werebear which engulfed him at once.

Azure, atop Micky, led the way to the northern side of the mountain. She wasn't sure what the weredragons would do collectively to create a passage out of Lancothy, but if their ancestors had banded together to hollow out the mountain, she was confident these could create an exit.

The scene on the ground was fire and destruction. Figures streaked between houses, their hands waving frantically in the air. Had Monet and Ever gotten to the officials? Creating a way out of Lancothy wasn't going to get everyone to safety if the wereanimals didn't get there in time.

The burgundy carriage, encrusted with bits of gold streaked across the sky. Oak sat nobly on the front with two dragons pulling it. It arched toward the city center, moving as fast as a comet. The dragons raced, hungrily on a mission.

Timber and Ronalds, Micky said in Azure's mind. *They're devoted to a peaceful end to this, even if that involves some violence.*

"Isn't that counterintuitive?" Azure asked.

Unfortunately sometimes violence can bring about peace, but it should be a last resort.

Something blurred at the edge of Azure's vision. One of the weredragons dove toward the ground and fire shot from his mouth, set fire to the path three werewolves had taken. She hoped it would be enough to keep the werewolves away from the wereanimals. The curse wouldn't be broken until they exited the mountain, so timing was crucial. How had it come down to either being buried in a mountain or risking being eaten alive as they ran for freedom?

"It's a rush up here, isn't it?" a familiar voice asked by Azure's ear.

She whipped her head around, at first only seeing a blur of black. Azure sucked in a breath, thinking it was a bat, but then she saw the raven clearly.

"Manx!" she called in relief.

"The one and only," he said, then rose and darted to the far southern corner. Over his shoulder he called, "I've gone batty!"

A colony of bats shot toward Azure, and Manx flew through the swarm to break up their formation. The bats turned and followed the pooka like he was their long-lost leader.

"We might be all right after all," she said to herself as Micky flew to the northern side of the mountain, but then Azure's gaze dropped to the ground and with it her heart.

As Micky drew closer Azure could make out two figures she recognized from New Egypt. One was the vampire who had taken her to Hamilton and Cordelia, and the other was the one who had come after her when she'd tried to escape.

Fuck! This can't get any worse, Azure thought. They needed a break.

Just then a booming voice filled the air, magically amplified for all to hear.

25

The shaking wereturtle held the wand up to his mouth as he peered over the edge of the highest building in Lancothy. He cleared his throat, and the sound reverberated over the land. "Citizens of Lancothy, the mountain will soon implode." The wereturtle's voice trembled, and he looked at Ever and Monet for support. Both nodded to encourage him to continue. "We have always stayed inside our homes after sunset, but tonight we must ignore that rule and brave the werewolves. Please come out of your homes and go to our northern border. The time has come for us to leave our land."

Ever watched as wereanimals exited their homes. Most looked around disoriented, and some had been bruised by the tremors. They stumbled through the streets in bewilderment, but to his relief they headed for the northern border.

The two dragons and the carriage landed on the top of the building, and Ever shuffled the wereturtles toward it.

"Get in!" he urged them. The three wereturtles looked confused, but Monet already had the carriage door open and he ushered them inside.

The first hesitated when he stumbled into the carriage. "Yes, yes, it's bigger on the inside. Gawk later. Mountain imploding, remember?" Monet said, pulling him to the side to make room for the rest.

When they were all in the carriage, Ever leaned out the door. "We're ready. Let's go pick up some more wereanimals, Oak."

"Hold on tight," Oak said, flicking the reins.

Using the carriage to pick up the wereturtles had been genius on Oak's part, since the slow-ass wereanimals would never have made it out otherwise. The carriage could easily hold fifty or so wereanimals, ensuring that more got to safety in time. The mountain was rumbling louder than before—they really couldn't get out of Lancothy one moment too soon.

Laurel ushered a group of weresnakes to a corner and showed them the best path to the northern border. Finswick joined her, having directed other wereanimals who were lost where to go.

"We can't leave. This is our home," a wererabbit said, holding on to the doorframe of his house. His wife and kids yanked at his arms and legs.

"Come on, Papa. We have to get out of here," one of the smaller wererabbits cried, pulling one of his ears as her siblings continued to try and drag their father away.

"N-n-no. I refuse," he stammered.

Laurel cast one last glance at the weresnakes, who seemed to be on the right path now, and hurried over to the wererabbit family. "Peter, I know that leaving Lancothy is scary, but you must."

The wererabbit stiffened as he looked at Laurel. "You! You're the traitor who left our land!"

"I'm most certainly *not* a traitor. I'm a free werecat, able to make my own choices, and I decided to venture outside this land. No one loves the wereanimals of Lancothy more than I do," Laurel said—and suddenly something unlatched inside of her. The guilt she'd been riddled with since leaving Lancothy fell out of the box inside her where she'd buried it. She released it with a breath and continued, "Leaving Lancothy will be scary, I'll admit, but the world outside this mountain is beautiful and rich, and full of so much diversity."

"Diversity! Is that what you're calling the prejudice that we'll suffer outside our land?" the wererabbit shouted as another tremor ripped through the town, making them all jostle into one another.

"Yes, I'll admit that when we leave here that witches, wizards, humans, Light Elves, and all sorts of others will stare at you, but that's mostly our ancestors' fault. Wereanimals have rarely been seen on Oriceran for hundreds of years. They'll stare at us because we're different to them, and our appearance is new to their eyes. But you know what?"

Laurel paused, waiting for his reply to her baited question.

"What?" the wererabbit obligingly grumbled, still

clutching the doorframe although his family had stopped pulling on him and were facing Laurel.

"You're going to stare right back at them, because I'm here to tell you that they look funny." Laurel stooped to look at the youngest wererabbit. "Do you know that gnomes don't have a single bit of fur on them?"

The little wererabbit's eyes widened. "Why not?"

Laurel shrugged. "That's just how they were made. They're unique, and very different from us." She straightened and looked at the whole family. "And you know what else? Gnomes are lovely. They're intelligent, ornery, and have a subtle humor that you'll miss if you're not careful. But if you stay inside Lancothy, you'll never meet a gnome. You'll never meet anyone, because this mountain is on its way down."

"Come on, Peter," the mother wererabbit urged. "We will make a fine home outside Lancothy."

"I daresay you'll make one that's better than your old one, but you need to hurry," Laurel said as the ground rumbled like the stomach of a hungry giant.

"Okay, fine, I'll leave," Peter said, releasing the doorframe and scrambling away from the house.

Laurel let out a huge breath as the dragon-powered carriage landed in the middle of the lane, the wide girth of the burgundy carriage shrinking to fit the narrow road. Ever flung open the door and waved them in. "Come *on*! We're almost full, and we have to go."

The wererabbits scurried for the carriage and the children let out gasps of surprise after entering. "It's bigger on—"

"Yeah, yeah," Monet could be heard saying inside.

"Stand against the back wall, and stay away from my vodka."

When the family had disappeared into the carriage, Ever gestured to Laurel and Finswick. "Come on!"

The cat sprinted up the stairs and disappeared into the carriage, but Laurel stayed in place and shook her head. "No, I'm going to check more of the homes. I have to ensure everyone gets out."

"Be fast," Ever said, looking up at the top of the mountain. "We don't have long."

Laurel nodded and raced down the road.

A crowd of wereanimals wer already heading for the northern border. Azure flattened herself against Micky's neck to help her optimize her speed. Beside her Hoarfrost and Lightning flew, and the other weredragons followed them.

Micky angled down toward a grassy green field. Azure had no idea what the weredragons could do collectively to create an exit, but if they were the ones who had hollowed out the giant mountain then she had no reservations about their ability to make a hole in the side of it. The mountain continued to thunder and large boulders rained from the walls, exploding when they hit the ground to send debris everywhere. The wereanimals scattered to avoid the wreckage.

Micky landed as the carriage pulled by Timber and Ronalds left the exploding city, where fires had engulfed the ruins of the buildings. Azure swung her leg over Micky's side before the dragon had even landed.

When she heard wereanimals screaming, Azure spun. The situation she'd been dreading played out in front of her eyes. A pack of werewolves raced toward them, their teeth bared and yellow eyes glowing. They were fifty yards from the closest group of wereanimals.

"No!" Azure yelled. The carriage was still too far away, and wouldn't be there in time. Azure turned to Micky, but knew that the dragon couldn't help. She was with the weredragons, who were standing in a circle collecting energy.

Azure pulled out her wand, trying to remember which spell she could use from that distance. The werewolves were bounding forward so fast that they'd be on the first set of wereanimals at any moment.

The group screamed and tripped over their own feet trying to flee. Fear could be a motivator, or as in this case, it could cause mistakes.

Azure ran toward the wereanimals and werewolves. She had to do something. Just then a lone dragon darted from the sky, fire scorching from his mouth. He blazed a wall between the wereanimals and the wolves, and shrieks told Azure that some of the werewolves had been burned.

She wasn't granted a moment to breathe, however…the mountain shook more brutally than ever before.

Most of the wereanimals fell, and more sharp rocks showered down. A large chunk of the mountain broke off from overhead and plummeted to the grass, digging a jagged hole and nearly obliterating a group of weresheep.

The carriage landed and Ever swung the door open, his

eyes scanning the crowd until they found Azure. His relief immediately wrote itself across his face and he hopped down from the carriage, pushing back the wereanimals who were trying to exit. He hurried to her, ducking to avoid the dust and dirt that sprinkled from above.

"What's going on?" he asked.

Azure pointed to the weredragons and Micky. A glow had started to burn between them, and it was slowly spreading to the center of the group. "We're waiting for them to open a hole."

"How long will it take?" Ever asked, but then he shook his head. He realized she didn't know the answer. How could she?

The third of Oak's dragons continued to fly back and forth, keeping the werewolves at bay, but the standoff wouldn't last long. One had already found a way around the wall of fire and was pacing up the side of a hill with a hungry look in its yellow eyes.

"Is everyone out of the city?" Azure asked, almost vibrating. She couldn't take the wait any longer. There had to be *something* she could do.

"I think so. Laurel stayed behind to check, though," Ever told her.

"She *what?*"

"Finswick is safe in the carriage, but I didn't have time to argue with her about staying behind," Ever explained. "And you know this is important to her. Just as you had to save Virgo, Laurel needs to save Lancothy."

Azure nodded. Ever couldn't have put that better.

And things couldn't be any worse, Azure noted, as bats swarmed toward them. Manx's tactics were apparently not working anymore. The dragon left the line of fire he'd been maintaining to go after the bats, and Manx dropped out of formation and flew under the dragon just as it let out a blast of fire. The bats dispersed, racing in different directions.

A small bit of relief swam into Azure's stomach when Manx hit the ground in stallion form and raced over to her. His beam-like eyes shone, creating a hopeful light in the darkness of Lancothy. And then Azure noticed even more light—the weredragons' glow, now a huge orb, had been directed at the northern wall. Rocks fell from the wall and stacked up in giant piles as the entire mountain vibrated. More boulders crashed down, and Ever covered Azure's head against the flying debris. Trees groaned and keeled over throughout the field. It was coming. The end was here.

For a moment Azure believed she'd failed. All her bad decisions had led to this moment, where she destroyed the kingdom of Lancothy as well as ending her friends' lives. She held onto the arm around her head for a second, and then wrapped hers around Ever's waist. If she was going to die, at least it would be in his arms.

A loud crack, deafening thunder, and something as bright as lightning shot across her vision. She pulled her head away from Ever's chest, but was unable to see anything. Dust and smoke filled the immediate area. Coughing, Azure waved her hands in front of her face, and then she saw it—the light of the rising sun spilling through a giant hole in the side of Lancothy Mountain. It flowed through the cavity and bathed the hills and the wereani-mals who stood gasping for breath.

"Go now!" Azure commanded, as the mountain lurched under their feet. It was wide enough that several could exit at a time. The wereanimals spilled through one after another, many times stumbling when the ground under them trembled.

"Go! Go! Go!" Ever chanted as the dragons lifted the carriage off the ground. It soared out of the mountain.

The lone dragon made another fiery pass between the werewolves and the wereanimals. The one who had gotten around the barrier now looked down on them from the top of a cliff, and the morning light would be their only protection from him.

"Come on," Ever said, pulling on Azure's hand. The final wereanimals exited through the hole and the were-dragons and Micky lifted into the air, the last to leave besides Azure and Ever.

"But Laurel?" Azure stared back at the city, which was now completely ablaze.

"Maybe she was with the others," Ever stated, but he didn't sound confident.

"I can't leave her. What if she's still in the city?" Azure asked.

"Then there's nothing we can do. I'm sorry," Ever said, his eyes filled with remorse.

The top of the mountain began to crumble, and pieces of it fell into the middle of Lancothy. The greatest tremor yet sent Azure to the ground, and Ever with her. This was the end. She gave the city one last look, and crawled to the exit. Dust filled her lungs and a barrage of rocks assaulted her but she kept moving, Ever at her side. The fresh air and morning light kissed her nose and the top of her head as she watched the people of Lancothy speeding away from the mountain. Everyone was trying to get as far from it as possible, since it was just about to blow.

Azure scrambled to her feet and Ever grabbed her hand and they ran—ran as far as they could from the land that had trapped its people and was soon to be no more.

26

Lux and Devo were almost to the northern border, where the weredragons had opened a hole in the mountain. Sunlight spilled through the opening, but Lux didn't care. He'd risk the burn if they could just get past the line of fire.

Lux halted. *"Fuck!"*

"Are those—" Devo began, stumbling backwards.

"Werewolves," Lux hissed, his fangs now prominent.

The werewolves spun to face the two vampires and crouched, growling madly.

"What do we do?" Devo asked, his voice vibrating with fear.

"Just stay still. We have to find a way around them," Lux said.

"Around them? Fuck that, I'm running," Devo cried, and sprinted in the opposite direction.

The werewolves raced after him, and as they passed Lux jumped as high as he could and landed on the other side of the pack. He knew the flames would be lethal to him, but he had no choice so he sprinted through the wall of fire. It wasn't as thick as he had thought it was. The dumb mutts had been deterred by something so thin? Fuck, it burnt, but only for a moment. Lux stopped and slapped at his arm, which extinguished the flames immediately.

He turned back to the wall of flames. The dumbass dogs could have gotten through, but thankfully they hadn't. Poor idiot Devo was probably being devoured by the pack at this very moment. Lux turned back to the exit and let out a laugh. He was going to make it. He hitched the bag of bats over his shoulder as he was knocked off-balance by the great shuddering of the mountain. He'd made it to the exit just in time.

Lux strode cautiously forward, unable to run now due to the tremors under his feet, when a howl behind him made him freeze. He dared to turn and look over his shoulder. At the top of a short cliff was one of the werewolves, its yellow eyes on him.

As Lux sucked in a breath and whipped around to sprint for the exit, the sound of the werewolf launching off the cliff and tearing after him registered in his mind. He ran as fast as the terrain would allow, tripping many times over the buckled ground.

Teeth sank into Lux's calf, and a howl of pain ripped from his mouth. The venom of the bite burned more than anything he had ever felt. Lux spun around and punched the werewolf, then swung the bag of bats at the monster to make it let go of him. He pushed up to his good leg and leapt for the exit with the werewolf on his tail. Lux barreled through the hole, expecting the werewolf to follow him, but the beast didn't. It stayed inside the quaking mountain.

The sun wasn't all the way up yet but the light still burned, making the fire he'd leapt through feel like nothing. Lux spotted the wereanimals and the queen straight ahead, so he darted to the right to take the less traveled route away from Lancothy, and in the direction of a small cave. He needed to escape the sun and tend to his werewolf bite.

Laurel was running through the library when the ceiling caved in. She'd confirmed that the town had been evacuated, but had thought she had time for one last thing...the books. If she could just save a few of them, it would be worth the risk. There were volumes in the library of Lancothy that were one of a kind. That was what had brought the queen of Virgo here in the beginning—to retrieve the *Book of Branches*.

Laurel ran toward the exit with six books pressed to her chest. She knew what she'd find, but she still had to try. The door was blocked by the beams that had fallen, so her last remaining hope was to take the basement tunnels to the middle of the field. That was how she'd gotten Azure and Ever out of Lancothy the first time. The tunnels might have collapsed in the meantime, though.

The building rumbled as it fell apart, and smoke wafted through the air. Something was on fire—probably most of Lancothy. Laurel sucked in a breath and ran for the stairs that descended into the basement. The werewolves might get her or the mountain might crush her, but she had to try to get out.

―――――――――

Azure bent over, trying to will more oxygen into her lungs. She managed to take a giant breath, and straightened. She had too many things to do to spend time trying to catch her breath right now.

The weredragons stood in a group, wings extended and eyes on the mountain. Azure strode over to them, grateful to see Micky's kind eyes watching her.

"Thank you for what you did," Azure said to Hoarfrost. "It's because of you that the wereanimals are safe." She motioned to the horde of wereanimals who were trudging down the mountain toward...well, who knew where they were headed or what they'd find. Oak had landed the carriage, and more wereanimals were filing out. Finswick wove his way through the crowd barking orders.

Monet's voice could be heard over the commotion. "No pushing. And no, you can't take that vase. Come on, people...I mean, 'animals.'"

Hoarfrost bowed his head, and Azure saw a tiny man with a red nose and stocking hat hidden in the folds of his wing. Pedgit winked at her.

The weredragon looked at Azure. "I'm afraid we didn't save everyone, but we're grateful that you asked for our intervention. We would have departed too soon, and been left with many regrets."

"Not everyone?" Azure asked, spinning around. Laurel

should have come through by now, but she hadn't left with the rest of the wereanimals and she wasn't in the carriage. There were other groups spread out across the area, but she didn't see a werecat among them.

Panic constricted her chest, but the mountain thundered just then and a strong wind swept through the center and out its top, stealing her attention. A mushroom cloud erupted, blanketing everything with soot and dirt, and the mountain fell. A loud *crack* assaulted Azure's ears, and she dove beneath the advancing wave of smoke and dust that swept across the land. Where the mountain of Lancothy had stood seconds prior was only a mound of rock and dirt. It was gone.

Laurel! Where was she?

She turned to Ever with tears streaming down her face. "Did you see Laurel? Where is she? Do you think she made it out?"

Ever shook his head, pain filling his eyes. "I don't know, Azure."

"She can't be gone! She *can't* be!" Azure yelled, and then she felt something in her head. At first she thought it was Micky's voice, but this one was different—something that she'd always been connected to, although she hadn't known. When Azure closed her eyes, pictures streaked across her vision. The Howling Willow sent her images of events all over Oriceran that were happening at that moment. Azure drew in a long steady breath and allowed herself to sink deeper.

"Azure, are you all right?" she heard Ever ask, but she didn't answer. Instead, she scanned the images until she found one that filled her heart with hope...and also desperate fear.

Azure whipped open her eyes and shot toward the remains of the mountain, which were still settling.

"Where are you going?" Ever shouted, racing after her.

"To the chute."

"The chute? You mean, how we got out of Lancothy the first... Oh!" Ever said, understanding.

Azure didn't know how she'd recognize the random place where the chute came out of the neighboring mountain, but she didn't have to. The Howling Willow knew where she had to go.

As if frozen by an invisible force Azure halted and began digging, pulling away rocks and dirt until she found the wooden door. It was incredible that she'd located it when there were so many places she could have looked. The magic of the Howling Willow stole her breath.

With all her might she yanked the door open and peered into the chute. It hadn't caved in...but Laurel wasn't there. She closed the door and turned around, thinking she'd missed something.

Azure stood back up. "I don't understand."

"You thought she would be in there?" Ever asked.

"The Howling Willow showed me that she was, but it's empty," Azure told him.

"Maybe it was wrong," Ever said, shaking his head.

"Or maybe it gave you the vision a bit early," Monet said, striding over with his finger extended.

Azure looked back at the door as it moved, but only an inch, as something bumped into it. "Laurel!" Azure yelled, tearing the door open again.

There, battered and covered in dirt, was the werecat. Azure pulled her out and into her arms. "I was so worried you'd—"

Azure couldn't bear to finish her own sentence. Laurel turned back to the tunnel to retrieve something. "I'm sorry to worry you. I went back to get these," she said, pulling out several bound volumes.

"*Books*? You risked your life for *books*?" Monet yelled angrily.

Laurel gave them a smile, one so wide it lightened Azure's heart. "Oh, yes. There are a few things I will die to protect, and books are one of them. I lost my land, but freed my people. Lancothy will remember its history because it's all documented here."

Azure took the first volume from Laurel's hands and read the title: *Inside the Mountain We Find Peace: The Complete History of Lancothy*.

Azure looked at the mountain that was no more, the one that had shielded the wereanimals from themselves. Now they were free to bless Oriceran with their gifts. All would benefit from Lancothy's fall.

EPILOGUE

Cordelia looked up from the chessboard when something scratching at the door to the boarding school got her attention. She gave Hamilton a curious glance.

He lifted one of his black eyebrows. "Smells like Lux has returned."

Cordelia pulled in a breath. "But not Devo."

"No, I'm guessing he got himself in trouble," Hamilton said, making his move. "By the smell of it and Lux's ragged breathing, he's on death's doorstep."

"Well, currently he's on *our* doorstep. I truly hope he's not leaving blood all over the place," Cordelia said, snapping her fingers to summon a servant.

A woman wearing a maid's outfit and several bite marks on her neck stepped forward. "Yes, madam?"

"Go and let Lux in, and clean up any mess he's left behind," Cordelia ordered the woman she'd condemned to be their servant and snack.

"Yes, madam. Right away." The woman hurried toward the entrance.

"At least he brought us some bats," Cordelia said, considering her next move.

"Yes, and a decent number by the sound of it." Hamilton combed his hands through his white-streaked black hair. Cordelia wondered what Queen Azure's soul mark would be when they turned her into a Founder vampire.

It was always exciting to see where the mark appeared. She hadn't even found her own because it was on her back —that had been Hamilton. His soul mark, the white streak in his hair, was noticeable, and one of the things Cordelia found most attractive about her mate. He wore his mark as a soulless creature boldly. The sort-of- dagger-shaped birthmark on her back was noticeable only when she wore a backless dress like the one she presently had on.

Lux slammed into the doorframe of the large study. His face was badly burned, and blood dripped from his leg.

Cordelia blinked impassively at the follower vampire. "Where are the bats?" she asked coldly.

"I left them in the lobby." Lux stumbled forward and then fell. The leg of his jeans was ripped, and there was a bite wound on his calf. It was green and infected, and Cordelia turned away in disgust.

"You got yourself bitten by a werewolf," Hamilton said, shaking his head. Disappointment was strong in his voice.

"Master, I need your help. Please!" Lux begged.

Cordelia rolled her eyes and let out a long sigh. "And Devo? Where is he?"

"He's gone. The werewolves… And the mountain—it's gone too. I barely got out," Lux said, crawling forward and stopping a few feet away from the pair at the chess table. "I had to stay in a cave during the day. And this bite…"

Hamilton rose and extended an arm to Cordelia. She took it at once, allowing him to escort her around Lux. "At least you were able to get some bats, so you weren't a complete failure," she called over her shoulder.

"Masters, please!" Lux yelled.

Hamilton paused on the threshold to give Lux an impatient stare. "There is no cure for a werewolf bite. You'll be dead within the hour."

Cordelia turned to her mate with a wicked smile on her face. "But thankfully he returned with the bats before dying. Now, shall we prepare for our journey?"

"Yes. I'm very interested in seeing the kingdom of Virgo, where the witches and wizards are incredibly powerful," Hamilton said.

"They will make even more incredible vampires," Cordelia agreed.

"And then the queen will have no choice but to join us," Hamilton said, escorting Cordelia to the foyer, where the bats were squeaking loudly.

For my birthday this year, my friends reserved a spot at a RV park in Malibu. They love to glamp. I don't camp and glamping is kind of lost on me. I love hiking, but want to return to my house at the end of the day.

I've already digressed. Apologies.

Anyway, my friends have a fifteen-year-old daughter who is a budding writer and one day will be writing circles around me. Sitting at the picnic table and overlooking the Pacific Ocean, Farah and I discussed books on my birthday. I was telling her about my upcoming book in Oriceran which would involve a werekingdom. She asked me what it was called. I told her I hadn't thought of a name yet and she ought to come up with one. For the rest of the weekend, Farah thought on this and when it was time to depart she said, "Lancothy. That's the name I've chosen for the werekingdom."

And so that's how Lancothy was born. I remember its inception as part of my birthday celebration, hence the story and unnecessary details. I'm hoping that one day when Farah's a famous author, she will tell her fans that she named the nobel prize-winning book called, "Lancothy."

Hey, I can dream, right?

I get all my best ideas from others. For instance, we can thank the brilliance that is Tim Adams for the weredragons. He and Alastar Wilson had a lengthy conversation on how the weredragons should look and how their abilities would manifest. We can thank them for coming up with the color connection to the weredragon's abilities.

Lisa Frett gets is all of the credit for Pedgit, right down to naming the drunken brownie. She has great ideas when it comes to my books. Lisa, seriously, keep them coming.

Micky Cocker is a prized resource who I couldn't do this without. She gives me lists of names for characters that haven't been used in KGU or Oriceran books. And Micky did become the trusty dragon bodyguard. I didn't plan that in the beginning. Actually, I was trying to come up with the name for the dragon in book five and the name Micky popped into my head. I realize now that the universe was saying, "Ask Micky for a name." I misread the message from the universe, as I tend to do, and named the dragon Micky. I have no regrets. She's a masterful dragon. And you might have noticed that I named two other dragons after superfans, Tim Adams and Ron Gailey. Those guys make what I do more fun.

As some of you know, I'm simultaneously writing this Oriceran series and in the Age of Expansion universe. It's making me feel like I have split personalities at times. I haven't slipped up and had Azure pull out her pistol yet, but I am thinking of having Ghost Squadron crash onto Oriceran. Then they can grab Blisters and take him to Onyx Station.

Thank you so much for reading, supporting and brightening my day with your comments and reviews. I read everything, although it's hard to always comment. I'm super grateful to write books and do what I love. You all make that possible.

Sincerely,

Sarah

Check out Sarah Noffke's Fantasy Series:

Vagabond Circus

A circus that is spellbinding, mesmerizing and deadly. When a stranger joins the cast of Vagabond Circus--a circus that is run by Dream Travelers and features real magic--mysterious events start happening. The once orderly grounds of the circus become riddled with hidden threats. And the ringmaster realizes not only are his circus and its magic at risk, but also his very life. Vagabond Circus caters to the skeptics. Without skeptics, it would close its doors. This is because Vagabond Circus runs for two reasons and only two reasons: first and foremost to provide the lost and lonely Dream Travelers a place to be illustrious. And secondly, to show the nonbelievers that there's still magic in the world. If they believe, then they care, and if they care, then they don't destroy. They stop the small abuse that day-by-day breaks down humanity's spirit. If Vagabond Circus makes one skeptic believe in magic, then they halt the cycle, just a little bit. They allow a little more love into this world. That's Dr. Dave Raydon's mission. And that's why this ringmaster recruits. That's why he directs. That's why he puts on a show that makes people question their beliefs. *He wants the world to believe in magic once again.*

AUTHOR NOTES - MARTHA CARR

WRITTEN FEBRUARY 12, 2018

I travelled to London recently for the 20Books conference where I got to meet a lot of authors and spend time outside of the virtual world. You might call that realm, 'reality'. Super fans of the Oriceran Universe like Micky Cocker and Peter McLean were also there and of course I had troll stickers in my pockets. (Thank you, Micky for the wonderful diorama of London to always remind me of the trip.)

At the end of the conference all the panelists were on the stage taking questions and the last question was, "What was your low point?" I knew instantly what my answer was to that and raised my hand because of where the story is right now and because it's a message we can all use on any given day. Things get better in ways we can't imagine.

My low point was in 2008 during that recession. Remember that giant whomp where it felt like we were breaking up with the economy and we'd beg the stock market to take us back but it just slid further away? I was a print journalist (because newspapers will never go away) in New York City (where Bernie Madoff was making things twice as bad) and was fielding calls from other journalists who were sure I'd be okay, so I could reassure them. Truth was I would eventually lose just about everything I owned (some sold, some given away) and would be left with 2 ½ chairs, a bed and a dresser. That was it.

Then in 2010, I was in a new city where I knew no one, still running lean, taking odd jobs and was diagnosed with terminal cancer – no insurance. I made a lot of phone calls and was turned down by a lot of doctors until I ran across this grant that normally took 6 weeks to get approved. Too long to save me and the surgeon said he wouldn't operate without approval.

But without asking me, a clerk walked my application from desk to desk and building to building and stood there, waiting till she got an answer – and in ONE DAY got it approved! She saved my life… literally.

Okay, fast forward to today and this new Universe with Michael Anderle and the wonderful stories from Sarah Noffke that grow and expand with each book. (A werekingdom!) This past month, I signed the contract for my dream house in Austin… 10 years later and it will take movers to get everything there even if a couple rooms will be empty for now.

You see? Things get better and magic happens. Really cool thing is I look back on that whole timeframe, and definitely don't want to do it again, and remember all the people around me (new friends nearby, old friends who sent me cookbooks and cinnamon – it was a thing then), and it's one of my favorite times. I was always surrounded by love.

It's a reminder to me to open up this new house and invite people in to share it with me. Make it a welcoming refuge for everyone. I'm looking forward with anticipation to all the new friends I'm about to make, including new SUPER FANS along the way. I'll keep my hands open to give and receive all of it.

And, one last thing... I'm grateful for this part of the journey with Sarah and Michael and all the other Oriceran authors that have become a family more than a business and that occasionally we all come together to celebrate outside of the virtual world in that weird place called 'reality'.

First, THANK YOU for reading our story, and our author notes (and publisher notes) here at the back of the book!

I'm going to take just a moment and talk about Micky Cocker as well.

Why? Because I just met her and her husband about nine days ago over in London, England.

Micky and her husband had driven over to an event my publishing company was putting on before the 20Books-To50k Indie Authors conference (which Craig Martelle orchestrated with his amazing amount of help) and it was the first time I had a chance to meet her in person

I was writing the Kurtherian Gambit series last year when Micky joined in to be a JIT reader to help out with finding those pesky as hell problems RIGHT BEFORE it goes out to the world.

And she did a wonderful job. Just because she was willing to help.

So much of what we do at LMPBN, and the help we

provide other indie author's is available because other's help us.

Micky went on to become a named character in Craig Martelle's books. As you read above, here in Sarah's books as well.

Now, I know that Micky's willingness to help, and do great things (and be freaking amazing) was all through a *virtual* relationship until I got to meet her in person. I would never have been able to meet her, if I hadn't created a Facebook group which helped other indie authors. That group put on a non-profit event in London, near enough to Micky's home for her and her husband to visit.

I have been pretty giving to others in my life. But, it took decades of helping others, to see the *FRUIT* of that helping turn around and help me like seeds planted in the ground. (Not that I wasn't blessed before, but I didn't count it 'pressed down, shaken together and running over' like it is now.)

It was like the Universe was storing up blessings in a *help-others* bank account until I could seriously use it.

I don't know about you, but decades is a *long* time to go believing that helping others would help you without seeing results (working on faith). I am aware of helping for the joy of helping.

However, I like to know that if I do X *then* Y will occur. If I'm told this and I believe this truth, then I want to see it HAPPEN.

I know it won't happen right away (generally speaking) but ... you know... I'm impatient.

Let's just say I believe for objective reasons at this point in my life.

Now, Sarah is taking the name (Lancothy) which Farah provided and placed it here into the book. I've no idea who Farah is, and I've never met her. However, if she were to ever be introduced to me, I would KNOW her story, and the effort she made to help name a Were Kingdom inside of our Oriceran Universe.

She helped, and now thousands of people who have read these author notes will know her name. I hope she does decide to write and publish stories, because she has already seeded her future with good things. And that help will (eventually) come back around and pay dividends.

Who knows? Maybe a future me, acting as a publisher, will be the lucky company to release her best seller?

I can hope.

Ad Aeternitatem,

Michael Anderle

- Rule of Magic (4) - Dealing in Magic (5) - Theft of Magic (6) - Enemies of Magic (7) - Guardians of Magic (8)

The Soul Stone Mage Series

* Sarah Noffke and Martha Carr *

House of Enchanted (1) - The Dark Forest (2) - Mountain of Truth (3) - Land of Terran (4) - New Egypt (5) - Lancothy (6) - Virgo (7)

The Kacy Chronicles

* A.L. Knorr and Martha Carr *

Descendant (1) - Ascendant (2) - Combatant (3) - Transcendent (4)

The Midwest Magic Chronicles

* Flint Maxwell and Martha Carr*

The Midwest Witch (1) - The Midwest Wanderer (2) - The Midwest Whisperer (3) - The Midwest War (4)

The Fairhaven Chronicles

* with S.M. Boyce *

Glow (1) - Shimmer (2) - Ember (3) - Nightfall (4)

ABOUT SARAH NOFFKE

Sarah Noffke, an Amazon Best Seller, writes YA and NA sci-fi fantasy, paranormal and urban fantasy. She is the author of the Lucidites, Reverians, Ren, Vagabond Circus, Olento Research and Soul Stone Mage series. Noffke holds a Masters of Management and teaches college business courses. Most of her students have no idea that she toils away her hours crafting fictional characters. Noffke's books are top rated and best-sellers on Kindle. Currently, she has eighteen novels published. Her books are available in paperback, audio and in Spanish, Portuguese and Italian. http://www.sarahnoffke.com

BOOKS BY SARAH NOFFKE

THE LUCIDITES SERIES:
Awoken, #1:

Around the world humans are hallucinating after sleepless nights.

In a sterile, underground institute the forecasters keep reporting the same events.

And in the backwoods of Texas, a sixteen-year-old girl is about to be caught up in a fierce, ethereal battle.

Meet Roya Stark. She drowns every night in her dreams, spends her hours reading classic literature to avoid her family's ridicule, and is prone to premonitions— which are becoming more frequent. And now her dreams are filled with strangers offering to reveal what she has always wanted to know: Who is she? That's the question that haunts her, and she's about to find out. But will Roya live to regret learning the truth?

Stunned, #2
Revived, #3

THE REVERIANS SERIES:
Defects, #1:

In the happy, clean community of Austin Valley, everything appears to be perfect. Seventeen-year-old Em Fuller, however, fears something is askew. Em is one of the new generation of Dream Travelers. For some reason, the gods have not seen fit to gift all of them with their expected special abilities. Em is a Defect—one of the unfortunate Dream Travelers not gifted with a psychic power.

Desperate to do whatever it takes to earn her gift, she endures painful daily injections along with commands from her overbearing, loveless father. One of the few bright spots in her life is the return of a friend she had thought dead—but with his return comes the knowledge of a shocking, unforgivable truth. The society Em thought was protecting her has actually been betraying her, but she has no idea how to break away from its authority without hurting everyone she loves.

Rebels, #2
Warriors, #3

VAGABOND CIRCUS SERIES

Suspended, #1:

When a stranger joins the cast of Vagabond Circus—a circus that is run by Dream Travelers and features real magic—mysterious events start happening. The once orderly grounds of the circus become riddled with hidden threats. And the ringmaster realizes not only are his circus and its magic at risk, but also his very life.

Vagabond Circus caters to the skeptics. Without skeptics, it would close its doors. This is because Vagabond Circus runs for two reasons and only two reasons: first and foremost to provide the lost and lonely Dream Travelers a place to be illustrious. And secondly, to show the nonbelievers that there's still magic in the world. If they believe, then they care, and if they care, then they don't destroy. They stop the small abuse that day-by-day breaks down humanity's spirit. If Vagabond Circus makes one skeptic believe in magic, then they halt the cycle, just a little bit. They allow a little more love into this world.

That's Dr. Dave Raydon's mission. And that's why this ringmaster recruits. That's why he directs. That's why he puts on a show that makes people question their beliefs. He wants the world to believe in magic once again.

Paralyzed, #2
Released, #3

REN SERIES:

Ren: The Man Behind the Monster, #1:

Born with the power to control minds, hypnotize others, and read thoughts, Ren Lewis, is certain of one thing: God made a mistake. No one should be born with so much power. A monster awoke in him the same year he received his gifts. At ten years old. A prepubescent boy with the ability to control others might merely abuse his powers, but Ren allowed it to corrupt him. And since he can have and do anything he wants, Ren should be happy. However, his journey teaches him that harboring so much power doesn't bring happiness, it steals it. Once this realization sets in, Ren makes up his mind to do the one thing that can bring his tortured soul some peace. He must kill the monster.

Note This book is NA and has strong language, violence and sexual references.

Ren: God's Little Monster, #2
Ren: The Monster Inside the Monster, #3
Ren: The Monster's Adventure, #3.5
Ren: The Monster's Death

OLENTO RESEARCH SERIES:
Alpha Wolf, #1:

Twelve men went missing.

Six months later they awake from drug-induced stupors to find themselves locked in a lab.

BOOKS BY SARAH NOFFKE

And on the night of a new moon, eleven of those men, possessed by new—and inhuman—powers, break out of their prison and race through the streets of Los Angeles until they disappear one by one into the night.

Olento Research wants its experiments back. Its CEO, Mika Lenna, will tear every city apart until he has his werewolves imprisoned once again. He didn't undertake a huge risk just to lose his would-be assassins.

However, the Lucidite Institute's main mission is to save the world from injustices. Now, it's Adelaide's job to find these mutated men and protect them and society, and fast. Already around the nation, wolflike men are being spotted. Attacks on innocent women are happening. And then, Adelaide realizes what her next step must be: She has to find the alpha wolf first. Only once she's located him can she stop whoever is behind this experiment to create wild beasts out of human beings.

Lone Wolf, #2
Rabid Wolf, #3
Bad Wolf, #4

CONNECT WITH THE AUTHORS

Want more?
   Join the email list here:
   http://oriceran.com/email/
   Find the Oriceran Universe on Facebook:
   https://www.facebook.com/OriceranUniverse/
   Find the Oriceran Universe on Pinterest:
   https://www.pinterest.com/lmbpn/pins/

The email list will be a way to share upcoming news and let you know about giveaways and other fun stuff. The Facebook group is a way for us to connect faster – in other words, a chat, plus a way to share new spy tools, ways to keep your information safe, and other cool information and stories. Plus, from time to time I'll share other great indie authors' upcoming worlds of magic and adventure. Signing up for the email list is an easy way to ensure you receive all of the big news and make sure you don't miss any major releases or updates.

Enjoy the new adventure!

Sarah Noffke and Martha Carr 2017

Sarah Noffke Social

Website: http://www.sarahnoffke.com

Facebook: https://www.facebook.com/officialsarahnoffke

Amazon: http://amzn.to/1JGQjRn

Martha Carr Social

Website: http://oriceran.com/

Facebook:
https://www.facebook.com/ChroniclesofLeira/